THE
GHOST
CAT

THE
GHOST
CAT

ALEX HOWARD

BLACK & WHITE PUBLISHING

First published in the UK in 2023 by
Black & White Publishing Ltd
Nautical House, 104 Commercial Street, Edinburgh, EH6 6NF

A division of Bonnier Books UK
4th Floor, Victoria House, Bloomsbury Square, London, WC1B 4DA
Owned by Bonnier Books
Sveavägen 56, Stockholm, Sweden

A CIP catalogue record for this book is available from the British Library.

ISBN: 978 1 78530 448 4

3 5 7 9 10 8 6 4 2

Typeset by Data Connection
Printed and bound in Great Britain by Clays Ltd, Elcograf S.p.A.

www.blackandwhitepublishing.com

For Sasha

"A cat has nine lives. For three he plays, for three he strays and for the last three he stays."

– Old English Proverb

Chronology of
Hauntings

A rare opportunity to acquire 7/7 Marchmont Crescent, a home of DELIGHTFUL APPOINTMENT and SPLENDOUR, entirely sheltered from the west wind.

4 July 1880. Messrs McCreadie and Company are proud to present flat 7/7 Marchmont Crescent, a virtuoso example of the architecture of DAVID BRYCE.

With two sleeping chambers, a grand parlour and INDOOR SANITARY CONVENIENCES THROUGHOUT, 7/7 Marchmont Crescent is a delightful choice for the gentleman of business, bachelor or lord and lady of leisure.

Each chamber has been exceptionally appointed and includes a range of features necessary for the employment of housekeepers, including DISCRETE SERVANT QUARTERS, fully equipped COOK'S RANGE, a scullery with ample storage and a SIX-POINT SERVANT SUMMONING SYSTEM. The flat also includes an unusual array of ornate finishes, detailing and plasterwork, including ebony handles, knobs and escutcheons and BRASS DOOR FURNITURE THROUGHOUT. Running water and gas connection included.

Situated on the third floor, the flat enjoys glimpses of the extraordinary ARTHUR'S SEAT AND CRAGS to the east and the BRAID HILLS to the south. The lounge includes a cornice moulded in the traditional SCOTTISH BARONIAL STYLE, deep skirtings, and bay window. The two chambers include fireplaces, servant call points, door architraves and built-in cupboards.

Horses and carriages may be lodged at the nearby Thirlestane Stables, 500 yards to the south, out of the way of noise and nuisance.

An initial payment of £12 deposit required*

*And £15 per annum repayment, thereafter, for fourteen years.

Prologue, 1902

THE *TICK-TICK* OF MR CALVERT'S wrist chronometer echoed through the wide living room of 7/7 Marchmont Crescent. Rousing from sleep, Grimalkin's ear twitched with each *snick* of the second hand. The morning light from the bay window caught the edge of his flank, which overhung the chair slightly, and was marmalade-coloured and turning glossy in the way of all cats who are reaching their older years.

All around the lounge, furniture and paintings began to take shape in the morning light. In the bay window stood a fine oak table displaying two urns in a flecked gold and Blue Willow design that loomed proudly over the room like a pair of guarding soldiers. On the opposite side to Grimalkin's chair, above the fireplace, was a huge oil painting of a mountain ravine that hung from chains on a picture rail. If you eyed it closely at this early hour of the morning (and Grimalkin often did), you could

1

even see it swaying as the first horses *clop-clop-clopped* along the street below, their cartwheels juddering over the cobbles and their milk churns jingling like bells.

Grimalkin opened an eye. A key had entered the lock in the front door. He raised his head and looked over before checking the hands of his master's chronometer.

My, she is six and twenty minutes late! he thought, arching his back into a dusty beam of sunlight making its way across the living room. He knew her schedule acutely: in a few minutes, she'd be lighting the fire in the master's back bedroom and would then head to the kitchen to set about fuelling the range for breakfast. It had been the same for years, ever since she served his master back in the old flat on Clerk Street. The tang of beeswax polish, Eilidh's trademark scent, came wafting into the living room as his forepaws clenched into the cushion velvet sending little sprouts of horsehair bursting free.

A whispering voice crept through a crack in the lounge door: "Mornin', wee Grimalkin! Mornin', ya gorgeous wee puss, puss, puss." Grimalkin slunk down to the floor and pawed his way slowly out to greet Eilidh the charlady, his companion and favourite human on earth.

"Come, come, puss, how are those aches today? Ooo, you like that wee scratch, eh? Shall we see what the dairyman left in the pantry, eh?"

Grimalkin craned his neck up into Eilidh's hand, licking off the coal dust from her palm, which this morning tasted oddly sweet and metallic.

A big throat clear came from behind one of the bedroom doors, followed by a cough and footsteps. "Ach, jings!" whispered Eilidh, before bustling down the hallway.

She'll be rebuked! thought Grimalkin. *The master has already risen, I can tell.*

He followed Eilidh into the back bedroom, where she had already begun setting the fire. On her knees crouching over the dust tray, Eilidh looked much more than her twenty-two years, her plump form and slightly curved back taking on the toil of the work she had begun as an apprentice char girl, in 1887, alongside her mother.

Back then, during the reign of Queen Victoria, Eilidh had found Grimalkin as a stray kitten on nearby Thirlestane Lane. Mewling for milk and nearing death in the corner of a stable, a mist, or "haar" as it is known locally, had swept across Edinburgh, causing Grimalkin's mother to abandon the site with the rest of her kittens. As he shivered in the urine-soaked straw, the haar had sunk its teeth into his minuscule bones, hour by hour. Another thirty minutes and the little cat would have been no more. The master of 7/7 Marchmont Crescent, Mr Calvert, a cartographer by profession, who was forever dressed in brown stockings and accompanied by a forbidding oak cane, had reluctantly agreed to keep the cat. In the early days of kittenhood, Grimalkin would often chase his tail on one of Mr Calvert's great maps that had been unfurled onto the study floor. Lost in the ecstasy of papery rustles, he would suddenly detect Mr Calvert's narrow head (bald apart from a few white wisps of hair on the side) looming over him. A moment of stillness would ensue, as Mr Calvert slowly placed his quizzing glasses over his eyes before releasing a sudden "Humph!", which would send Grimalkin charging off down the hall.

But Eilidh's face told a different story: big rosy cheeks flushed vivid red like a clutch of Scottish loganberries on her otherwise perfectly white skin. Her eyes permanently sparkled, as if she was always on the point of telling a joke, and their turquoise irises were so deep and kind one could tell, just by looking at them, that their bearer could be trusted with your secrets. She wore her black hair rolled up in a handsome pompadour, but despite her best efforts, it would often explode out of its frilly headdress in little corkscrew curls, making her look comic, and yet somehow charming. She was one of those people that always looked bright-eyed, and to Grimalkin she looked no different to the day in 1887 when she cupped him in her warm hand from the icy sodden straw of the nearby stable.

As Grimalkin padded over to the fire grate, which was just starting to lick with flames, he caught sight of his own reflection in Eilidh's brass firebox. A hunched tabby cat stared back at him, crooked of tail and jagged of whisker. His eyes, once lizard-green and flashing with alertness, were now, at fifteen years old, cloudy and drawn ever so slightly down at the corners, so that his pupils looked unnaturally large. To the unassuming passer-by, this might have given them a melancholy air, but, to the more perceptive among cats and humans, it in fact spoke of a profound and restless wisdom. His fur, at one time the envy of the neighbourhood for its dazzling mix of browns, marmalades and creams, was now flecked with white and constantly matted with bits of grit that he could never completely lick off. His forelegs were stout, with big paws, the likes of which would not seem out of place on one of his wildcat cousins, excepting his neatly rounded toes; and his ginger hind leg, once his proudest attribute when prowling the communal gardens, had now turned a deep fox-red and was bent in a half-curve that he couldn't straighten out. There was a majesty about him, as there is with all handsome cats grown old, and a robustness to his form that suggested a prodigious Victorian diet of lark pie, pork suet and dripping. He was a thinking cat and, as such, enjoyed a life of quiet intellectual contemplation.

But on this morning in September 1902, his whole frame, from the ends of his ear peaks right down to his tail, was lashing with pain. His leg joints throbbed, taking his mind plain off any thoughts of stalking for mice; and even now, as Eilidh placed his morning bowl of fish ends down on the pantry tiles with a familiar clatter, his ear did not twitch. Instead, he sat staring into the grate deeper and deeper, as the orange flames licked in between the knuckles of coal, his senses dulling and his mind becoming ever more silent.

No, this will not do! he thought, in a sudden rallying of mental strength. *A dreary soul doth guddle nay mice. I must still wash myself. A good ablute always puts me to rights.*

You see, even at fifteen, Grimalkin believed, as did many Victorian cats, that a clean pelt led to a pure soul. Rising, he padded closer to the fire, coming to rest on a little rug beside Mr Calvert's gramophone, which stretched up its huge brass trumpet like an oversized daffodil. But no sooner had he dampened his paw with his tongue and hooked it over his left ear than his muscles seized, and his tummy cramped with a pain so strong that it almost made him cry out loud.

No, I cannot. I simply cannot.

It is an alarming day when a cat can no longer wash himself. It signals the last of dignity and the end of choice. Feeling quite alone, Grimalkin squatted on the rug and decided to watch the skirl and twist of the flames again. As they flexed and grew, he thought back across his life. Being born in 1887, he had seen a lot ... the opening of the great Forth Rail Bridge, the first motion picture camera, the proliferation of works of literature by Robert Louis Stevenson and Mr Dickens ... the continual irrevocable rise of the steam train. *I have had much fortune ...* he thought as various memories panned up in his mind. *I have been well-kept, well-fed and well-groomed. Why, if a cat has nine lives, reserved for misadventure and poor luck, I dare say I am still on my first ...*

"Acht, you puir wee soul!" whispered Eilidh, re-entering the room. Grimalkin felt her warm hand come down on his head. "Ah, my darlin' wee puss, nay breakfast this mornin'? Not hungry? I'll bring yer victual in here for you, how about that? You stay warm and coorie by the fireside – only the cosiest for a wee moggy 'o yer vintage, puss, eh?"

Grimalkin nuzzled into Eilidh's hand, breathing in the warm coaly scent of her petticoat. "Aww, yes, yes, yes, yes, yer lovely wee moggy . . . Here, snuggle down, snuggle down. That's right. Have your breakfast later. You quite cosy? You rest up!"

She crouched down and kissed his head as the orange flames in the grate turned red and hot.

Grimalkin looked up at Eilidh. Her sparkling eyes and rosy face appeared streaky in his vision. He purred a long, laboured purr and curled himself into a tight ball against her stockinged calf on the rug.

"Thar, thar," whispered Eilidh, tickling his head. She rose, gathered her brushes in one hand, then, lifting her petticoat with the other, shuffled out into the corridor.

In the silence, Grimalkin's eyes closed. And under the strengthening morning light coming in through the part-opened shutters, the crackle of the fire and the warming smell of coal dust, his head fell silent, and the worries and travails that inflict all cats during their short time on this earth receded as if carried downwards on a tumbling vortex of sand. The ache of his back eased; the arduous pull and heave of his lungs subsided, and as the rising flames beat their warmth upon his fur, the twist of his thoughts fell silent for the last time ever in this life.

Cat-sìth

THE FIRST THING GRIMALKIN SENSED was a soft mist against his nose.

A little later, the gentle *shhhhhhhhhh* of cascading water swept around his ears and seemed to wash right through his soul. It filled him with great calm. Around this time, he felt the throbbing, arthritic pain that had nested in his spine for so long gently dissipate, as if floating into the mist. Then, in front of his eyes (if indeed he was *seeing* through his eyes) daubs of lemon-yellow light began to glitter and dance like ocean waves on a sunny day.

Is this paradise?

After a time, this yellowness began to split apart, breaking off into white ribbons which gave rise to a memory of home: the thin wisps of smoke that rose off bonfires in the communal garden of Marchmont Crescent, on frosty autumn mornings.

Is this what the afterlife feels like? What is that gushing sound? I want to see that sound!

Slowly, the twisting light began to form into objects and shapes.

He was sitting on a forest floor of dank leaves and moss. In front of him, within pouncing distance, was an enormous water-fall plunge pool. Something about the water was peculiar; instead of gushing away downstream, it stood mirror-flat and glittered with a carpet of multi-coloured sparkles as if it was alive. It stung Grimalkin's eyes to stare at it, and the coloured sparkles continued to jump and glitter on the back of his eyelids after he shut his eyes in pain. The violence of the huge column of water hitting the plunge pool was so intense that all the surrounding air was filled with spray, making the nearby rocks appear soft-focused. Peering ahead, Grimalkin fancied he saw the forms of ancient beasts appearing and disappearing in the waterfall's great hissing tongue, but he couldn't be sure. His mind felt numb, as if he was dreaming. And yet something about the chill of the mizzle on his face and the sponginess of the moss under his belly assured him that he was not. He was in another world. This was his new existence.

Ferns sprouted from cracks where little sub-streams of waterfall channelled between lumps of rock like blood through arteries. For a cat who had never ventured beyond the perimeter of a sealed tenement garden, the scale of these surroundings felt terrifying. Frightened, little Grimalkin lowered his belly into the moss, his eyes peering upwards in nervous expectancy.

Then, to his left, something glimmered. A stone plinth rose out of the undergrowth like a great tree stump.

What in the name of . . . ?

And on the plinth was a chair; an enormous and very peculiar chair. One thing was certain – it was definitely *not* made from oak with a horsehair cushion and velvet covering like the chairs Grimalkin was used to. Instead, it appeared to be made from twirling fronds of golden ivy. It was a forbidding, spiky edifice lurking there, half concealed in the mist, and something about it made Grimalkin's stomach knot in fear. Suddenly, as Grimalkin gazed at it, the forest canopy parted above him, letting down a great bar of light.

"M-rrow. M-rrooooooooooooow."

What's that? Hullo? Anyone there?

Above the hiss of water, Grimalkin could detect a sort of faint, low, intermittent growling.

M-rrow. M-rrooooooooow.

There it was again!

He looked up. Nothing. Only the yellow light of the sun trickling between the leaves of the forest canopy. Maybe he was imagining it? But a cat is very attuned to the call of another cat; back in his youth, Grimalkin would easily detect the whines of a brewing cat fight, even if the conflict was many yards off and in the dead of night. It seemed now, in this afterlife (or whatever it was) that his sense of hearing had returned with the sharpness of his early youth.

Mrrrooooww?

This time, Grimalkin saw it.

At the pinnacle of the waterfall, where the rock overhung the plunge pool, and seemingly immune to the torrent of water gushing over its legs, a giant black cat paraded up and down. It was easily triple the size of any feline Grimalkin had ever beheld and yet bore all the features of a Scottish wildcat. This alone told Grimalkin it was of supernatural origins. Its only marking was a great white spot that shone out from its chest like a moon and was almost too bright to look at directly. It stared down at Grimalkin with its huge green eyes, its black pupils pulled into long slits, like some villainous creature of the underworld.

Dreadful apparition! thought little Grimalkin, his paws clenching against the moss and his ears flattened in terror. *Begone now! Get thee away.*

The cat continued to stare unblinkingly from the summit of the waterfall, before rising to a stand. As it did, its leg bones pushed tautly against its skin, forming awful cada-ver-like peaks of flesh about its shoulders. Turning in a circle, it doubled back along the waterfall's summit, before clam-bering down the glistening rockface with a strange, almost reptilian, ease. Unblinking himself, and gripped by fear, Grimalkin watched the creature approach, hoping the carpet of fern would conceal his location. But it was futile. The beast had already seen him. It was heading right his way.

The beast half-walked, half-slithered up onto the golden throne, its legs and undercarriage disappearing in the swirling mist that encircled its base. All the while, its slit-pupiled gaze remained locked on Grimalkin, its head swiv-elling like an owl's as it maintained its unbroken stare.

Finally it took a seat on the throne, much like any cat would, with its rear flat against the golden base, and its huge forepaws held together like a pair of columns on a Grecian temple. It was definitely a cat, Grimalkin was certain of this, for now he could see its humongous whiskers and tail that stretched out so long and wiry that they could almost be mistaken for one of the many fibrous roots that spiralled out from the nearby bushes. The white heart on its chest, now truly vivid and bright against its velveteen fur, continued to pulse and glow as a heart would (if indeed this beast even *had* a heart) and its chest rose gently up and down. The thing was breathing. Just like Grimalkin.

Unearthly spectre! What could you want with me? This meek, poor, defenceless beast that so shudders under your lizard stare? thought Grimalkin, his fur spiked up.

"Silence!" thundered the great feline suddenly. To his astonishment, Grimalkin was shocked to discover he could hear his own thoughts out loud in the presence of this beast. He could, in other words, speak in much the same way as a human being. Speaking always seemed pointless to Grimalkin; like all cats, he had always been able to express everything he needed perfectly well in tail-flicks, purrs, chirrups and rubs; and any human worth their salt, like Eilidh, was able to understand this language. It was a happy, calm mode of communication, much unlike the shrieking voice-pollution insisted on by so many dunderheaded humans.

"Cursed Cat-sìth, you fool!" boomed the great feline suddenly. Grimalkin felt his little heart thump against his ribcage. The beast rose and circled the throne irritably before reassuming its gold seat. "For a mere *trifle*, I turn my back as Agnes McPherson from Shetland attempts to summon me in a triple cat-burning Samhain[1] ritual. Three precious seconds *and I go and miss a death.* You FOOL, Cat-sìth!" As the huge animal spoke, its very words seemed to set the ground trembling like an earthquake.

Grimalkin stared incredulously at the beast's mouth as it rose and fell like a human's, its huge eyes, now green and bulbous like limes, glimmering as it spoke.

"And now," said the beast, craning its horrific head towards Grimalkin, "I have gone and let a feline die unnecessarily ... "

Grimalkin retracted his neck as it neared. A stench of burning filled the air. Grimalkin felt like a pea – tiny and puny beneath this great hulk of fur and fire; though it was with great relief that the huge cat showed no outward signs of wanting to harm Grimalkin as it inched ever closer, bringing its nose within swiping distance of the little tabby's whiskers.

---

[1] Agnes McPherson from Scalloway, Shetland, whose failed attempt it was to summon Cat-sìth on 4 September 1902, later died in a house fire on Samhain Eve along with her twelve cats. Local legend maintains that several uncanny cat shrieks could be heard from the neighbouring villages of East Voe and Burwick as the green flames licked the house.

"Tell me!" said the beast suddenly, rising to its feet and towering over Grimalkin. "How many lives have you expended?"

Umm ... Lives?

"Louder!" roared the beast with another impatient flick of its tail that sparked crimson as it glanced at the stone plinth. "How many earthly lives have you expended?" The great cat leaned forward and softened its voice to a near-whisper. "All cats have nine lives on planet Earth – three lives when they *stay*, three when they *stray* and three when they *play*. Every earth-dwelling feline knows his place within this timeless incantation of cat-law. Do not play ignorant with me! WHAT LIFE ARE YOU ON, CAT?"

Pardon me, I do not wish to vex you, sir! stuttered the little cat, cowering so low he was positively at one with the fern. *Umm ... Well, I was born in 1887, so ... that makes me in my fifteenth year and ...*

"This was not the question Cat-sìth asked," interrupted the huge feline, snaking its body up the plinth and crouching its terrible fleshy haunches down on the gold throne, like a sphynx outside a pyramid. "I shall not ask again. How much misadventure have you endured during your time on Earth? Have you fallen from any great heights? Eaten a blot of underdone beef? Been hit by a pony and trap? There must be something that summoned you into my dominion ... "

Oh, stuttered Grimalkin. *N-none of that. I have had no misadventure. I have been most fortunate. I was t-taken in by a wonderful human called Eilidh early in my life and I have been*

15

p-privileged. I've only been allowed in a communal back garden, but no further. So no accidents with p-p-ponies and traps. I've dined on suet and pheasant and occasionally live rodent ...

A relief came over Grimalkin as the huge cat seemed to fall into a state of calm, listening to the details of the story attentively with closed eyes. At several parts of Grimalkin's speech, the white heart of the cat's chest throbbed and glowed especially brightly, forcing the little feline to close his eyes and wince from its glare.

"Humph," intoned the beast, looking askance into the waterfall. "There must be *something*. No accidents? No plunges from windows or fateful encounters with cyanide-laced macarons?"

Good gosh, no!

"Then why ARE YOU HERE?" roared the cat.

I don't know, I know not, sir, I know not! Please, tell me what I must do. I suppose I am becoming infirm ... fifteen ...

"Pah," snorted the cat. "Nothing for a privileged feline on a diet of pheasant. Recant the morn of your death ... "

A silence fell. Out of the corner of his eye, Grimalkin noticed the cat's great tail twitch left and right at the tip. It was waiting for a response.

Ummmm, said Grimalkin. *It was a normal morning, sir. Eilidh – the agreeable lady whom I mentioned – arrived to set the fire. I had my usual aches and pains. I greeted her. She left for ...*

"How did you greet her?" asked the cat, clenching its claws against the golden throne with an unpleasant scraping sound.

Oh, in the usual way, sir! I proffered a double hand rub and a triple ankle slide-past. Gave her palm a small lick too, as is often my want when there is coal dust there. I find the taste agreeable, you see . . .

"Hmmmm," said the beast in thought. "A double hand rub and a triple ankle slide-past. A typical feline greeting. And there was no strange flavour about her hand?"

Umm, no, replied Grimalkin. *It was, I attest, a little sweet perhaps . . . Perhaps as if there might be some sugar present among the soot. Nothing of concern, though.*

"Ahhhhh. Lead . . . " said the cat in one long purring breath. "A case of lead poisoning. I hear it is sweet on the tongue. A common cause of dispatch among your kind. I have awarded many an extra life to a feline whose mistress has removed leaded paint from the brasses or procured a lead-based unguent or ointment. The humans call us vain but, to be sure, they are the vainest species of all. And with you of ailing and advancing years, it was doubtless enough to stop your heart."

Grimalkin felt a little throb of fear and sadness. Could this be the case? If so, how tremendously awful his Eilidh must feel if this was the cause! He calmed himself with the knowledge that his death had been quick, and most plausibly put down to age, given Eilidh's knowledge of his growing infirmity about the legs and spine.

Beside him, the waterfall continued its deafening plunge, its spray curling into the boulders that flanked it like phantoms.

"I am in trouble," resumed Cat-sìth, rising and pacing off the throne through the gouts of mist. It continued to walk up and down through the fern, like a lion in captivity deep in thought. "I am in profound trouble. You see, old Grimalkin ... I have gone and let you die."

Watching the hulking figure musing on its recent past gave Grimalkin a strange, panicked feeling, as if something had gone wrong in the matrix of his existence that couldn't be righted, and might force him to reside in this steamy strange forest for all eternity.

Sh-should. Um. Do you want me to do something about it ... sir?

"No," breathed Cat-sìth quietly, its talon-claws flexing and retracting from its dragon-like feet. "It is Cat-sìth's error, and therefore Cat-sìth must make amends. I have never missed a death before. There must be something extraordinary about you, Master Grimalkin ... "

The brightness of the white spot on the great feline's breast caught Grimalkin's eye again. Suddenly he noticed, on closer inspection, that it wasn't a white spot of fur but a swirling gyre of glittering water.

"You are entitled to your nine lives, but I cannot return you to life. Such is decreed by the ancient proverb that under-pins the existence of all cats on this planet." The cat drummed its claws, one after the other, clearly in thought.

Suddenly, the creature rose, its terrible bones pulling its flesh so taut that Grimalkin worried one or more might burst through its skin. The little tabby remained still, hypnotised into silence by a mixture of awe, terror and anticipation. Once again, the giant feline surveyed Grimalkin with a penetrating gaze from its lime-like eyes. The eyes then slid away and began to take in Grimalkin's form. It seemed to be reading him for some kind of clue, taking in the contours of his face, the slight downward slope of his eyes, his deep tortoiseshell markings and his marmalade flank.

"Yeeeees," said Cat-sìth finally, with a drawn-out sigh. "I see you are a cat of uncommon curiosity and insight. The finest of our kind." It swung its head in a sort of flippant manner, before becoming serious again. "Given this, I feel you must be compensated. Cat-sìth is going to enlist you with a choice in recompense. How would *you* see me put right my error? Do you wish to pass over to oblivion now, and be done with it all? The benefit of that is nothingness – eternal peace and sleep; the ultimate desire of any cat." At this point, Cat-sìth paused and gave a little melancholy gaze at the waterfall. "Or … do you wish to return to planet Earth, and spend your remaining eight lives observing its future? But be warned!" said Cat-sìth suddenly. "While this option allows immunity from corporeal suffering of the body, it by no means guards you against the emotional sufferings *of the soul*."

Grimalkin listened, his brain working at double-speed. *You mean I am to … walk abroad? To dwell on?*

"If you choose this path," continued Cat-sìth, seeming not to hear Grimalkin, "you will no doubt experience a great many painful emotions. Fear, loss, heartache regret ... and many more positive ones besides. Your heart will contract, and while you may have some influence upon the fabric of the universe at the end of it all, I wager that you will eventually pass to oblivion, having done little more than fill your brain with the future accomplishments of the humans of this world. For despite our best efforts, it is the Human who rules this planet. You will see the future of humankind and all its great achievements and dismal failures. But one must question the uses of such a quest ... particularly for a mere cat like yourself."

Grimalkin thought for a second. His mind turned to the only source of love and connection he knew: Eilidh. His lovely Eilidh who brought him life and gave him a good home, food and love over those fifteen years. What would become of her?

I think I should like to go back, said Grimalkin with little hesitation.

"Very well," said Cat-sìth.

Grimalkin eyed the cat expectantly as the heart on its chest began to glow brighter than ever before, as if it were an extension to Cat-sìth's own mind.

"And naturally, your lives will be discharged according to The Cat With Nine Lives; namely, *for three he plays, for three he strays and for the last three he stays.* However, since no feline is ever allowed more than nine lives of any type, we must consider your first life completed. And since you were never allowed beyond the confines of enclosed gardens, we can consider this first life a *stay*-ing life. This leaves you two more lives in which you must *stay* within these confines. Thereafter, you are afforded to stray for three lives, followed by a final three in which you are permitted to play. All these lives, most unusually, are to be conducted with your existence in the supernatural realm. You are to be a Ghost Cat."

Grimalkin's mind raced with thoughts and questions. *So for my stray lives, I may leave my dwelling and venture far and wide?*

"Indeed," breathed Cat-sìth with a groan-like tone.

And for my play lives?

"For these," said Cat-sìth with a deepening tone, "you shall have the benefit of poltergeist capabilities. Your presence, while still invisible, may interact with the fabric of planet Earth to do what us cats pride ourselves in doing best: causing havoc, mischief and all kinds of unrecommended carnage. However you choose to employ these poltergeist capabilities is down to your good council and yours alone."

And how long am I to stay witnessing each age? enquired Grimalkin.

"Until you feel tired," said Cat-sìth. "When the pull of sleep falls upon your head, rest assured you will reawaken into your next life, in a new decade of the future." His gaze shifted down to his paws, a melancholy sense coming about him once more. "Of course, any emotional or intellectual learnings you may have gained over the years ... these will attend you in subsequent hauntings. You will be alone with these discoveries and feelings ... for better or worse."

And . . . And at the end of it all? said Grimalkin nervously.

"Ahhh." Cat-sìth, sighed. The white spot on his breast seemed to swirl and spin frantically in response to this question. For the first time, Grimalkin saw the beast close its eyes and bow its head as if in prayer. "That, my compeer, will be decided and revealed in its own good time."

A silence fell between them. Above, the clouds scudded quickly across the pale-yellow sky as the waterfall gushed in a continuous sheet, like the tail of a white horse. Grimalkin looked at the great feline with renewed awe as it lay draped across the throne, eyes still shut, as if in the grip of some kind of reverie.

Um . . . Cat-sìth, sir?

The almighty cat rose suddenly, walking past Grimalkin without a glance, before clambering up the mangrove-like vines that flanked the rocky outcrop of the waterfall. "I bid you good luck," it roared from the pinnacle of the waterfall. "And if you ever experience a world, years from hence, where the mysterious forms of my kind no longer hold the beliefs of mortals, remember unto that world the powers and presence of almighty Cat-sìth!"

Um, how do I get there?! mewled Grimalkin up the rockface, as the beast disappeared from view.

"Simply sleep! Fall to slumber now, and I grant that you shall reawaken in 1909 or I am not the King of the Cats!"

First Haunting,
April 1909

O N THE MORNING OF HIS first haunting, Grimalkin felt supple and alive; more alive, in fact, than he'd ever felt as a sentient breathing Victorian cat.

He had landed in 1909 with a thump. Rather than having to acclimatise his senses to the eerie, misty environment of Cat-sìth's waterfall, the transition through time felt immediate, as if he had been dropped from a huge height. Suddenly, he was just *there* ... sitting back on a fine oak table in the bay window of 7/7 Marchmont Crescent. With one turn of the head, he could see the whole street: there were the communal gardens opposite, tucked behind fili-greed iron railings and sweeping off to the right as the street disappeared into a tree-smudged infinity. It was clearly springtime as the trees opposite were bursting with taut little pods of pink blossom. Glimpsed at intervals along the street, the odd horse and carriage loitered while awaiting the emergence of passengers from tenement doors, their oil-painting-like stillness disturbed only when the horses tugged against the reigns or stamped on the cobbles with an irritated *clop*. Above, purple clouds huddled tightly, their edges yellow where the sun tried its best to pierce through. The cobbles were dark with the wetness of a recent shower. Grimalkin knew these showers well, having often bolted in from the garden when they struck, only to stare longingly out of this very window as the Edinburgh sun burst out again, making steam rise off the carriage tops below. It was a familiar and heart-warming scene; one Grimalkin could happily gaze at for hours in Victorian times, particularly if it was mating season and the pigeons were out on the sandstone sill, cooing and clucking tantalisingly close, almost within swiping distance.

Well, nothing has changed! thought Grimalkin suddenly, with a pang of disappointment. *That Cat-sìth charlatan has merely returned me to Victoria's reign! Why, I have been duped! Ah . . . ah, ah, steady on, wait . . .*

He turned his gaze back into the belly of the room. His eyes widened and his back fur prickled upwards in shock. Here, *everything* was different. In place of the sombre damask wallpaper of his Victorian youth, the walls had been painted a pure apple-green. Rather than great mirrors and huge paintings, little artworks studded the walls in clusters. Most of them appeared to feature the same fairy-like woman in billowing white robes. French? Dutch?

Grimalkin wasn't sure.[1] There was a soft hiss emanating from the room ... somewhere on the wall? Somewhere above? Grimalkin's ears twitched furiously. *Yes, there!* In the centre of the ceiling, the chandelier had been removed. In its place there hung a little brass sconce that breathed out an orangey flame behind a smoked-glass lampshade. Above it, the formerly pristine ceiling rose had turned black with tarry soot and Grimalkin could feel the dryness of the gas-heated air rasp at his throat.

They think they're being clever, he thought, eyeing the ceiling rose. *They will struggle to beat a good coal fire for efficiency and comfort!*

Fancy bow-fronted armchairs, settees and cabinets squatted about the floor, upon which books and papers were piled up into dubious little towers. On a side table, a looking glass and moustache comb rested beside an open snuff box. Apart from the flicker of the blue flame, everything was perfectly still as if frozen by some kind of spell.

Humph, apologies, Cat-sìth ... I see there HAS been a change ...

How can so much change in just seven years? Was Eilidh still tending the fires? It made Grimalkin feel eerie looking at it all: this room where he drew his final breaths had become a lens into the future. He was suddenly struck with the sense that this whole business of time travel might turn

---

[1] Most likely the early *Décor de la salle à manger* series of Art Nouveau works by Charles Rennie Mackintosh (1868–1928), a popular Scottish watercolourist and designer.

out to be rather more taxing on his brain than he'd initially thought.

But something else was different – Grimalkin himself. As he stood on the table, his paws perfectly centred, he became suddenly aware of a complete absence of pain. The arthritic throb in his back and legs had vanished. His left rear leg and flank, always a focus of curiosity to Marchmont Crescent's visitors owing to its bright marmalade hue, had lost its oily aged texture and become velveteen again, like a fox cub's tail. Down at the point where his paw hinged from the base of his leg, the little bald patch that had so long been the recreation ground for a particularly stubborn army of fleas was now smooth and itch-free.

Could it be that my ghosting role has rid me of the pestilence? If so, praise be!

Grimalkin rewarded the discovery with a wash. Gazing at the window pane, he was shocked to discover he couldn't see his reflection. However, as he rose and arched his back with ease, and felt the springiness of his ears as they pinged up each time he sent a damp paw across them, and glimpsed his perfectly pink toe pads, he could tell he had become young again. He couldn't see his eyes, but were he able to, he would have guessed that they were no longer rheumy and greyish, and that his whiskers were sharp and unjagged again. And he would have been right.

My word, I'm veritably juvenile! he thought, stretching up his tail like a broom handle. A potent, virile pride washed across him: he was a looker again, an Adonis of cats ... a youthful, muscular mouser whose iron claw had once commanded the envy and respect of all the cats in the neighbourhood. He rose to his paws and turned a large vainglorious circle on the table, his ears pricked up into sharp triangles. He leaped onto the back of an armchair, his supernatural paws making no noise whatsoever as they landed on the polished oak. He felt positively age*less,* neither kitten nor adult ... with all the vim and energy of the former but with the latter's acuity of mind.

I feel in the most capital of moods! May I be a spirit-puss FOREVER MORE!

Suddenly a noise. From over his shoulder there came the familiar creak of the living room door lock turning. Grimalkin spun round. A short, narrow-shouldered man entered the room in a silver-swirled Jacquard waistcoat. The man strode over to the bay window as if about to pull open the sashes, before turning back and making a sudden stop in the middle of the room, as if he'd been halted by a police constable. He then proceeded to bounce on the balls of his feet, his hands clenching and unclenching, and his eyes darting around the room frantically. At one point, he appeared to look directly in Grimalkin's direction, though could see nothing of him of course. What caught Grimalkin's feline attention most of all, however, was the perfect little moustache that crossed the man's top lip, its ends waxed up into points, like a mouse's tail. It seemed to jiggle in perfect time with the man's nervous energy as he bounced up and down on the spot. Stiffly, the man flopped down on the settee, placing one leg over the other with a dandy-like flourish, the fingers on his right hand patting a little ditty on the settee cushion, in an ongoing attempt to calm himself.

The man of the house? mused Grimalkin, for the man moved with the ease of a gentleman who knows he is unobserved in his own space; a rich man; an entitled man who has the wealth and means to live, by and large, as he pleases . . .

The man closed his eyes and let out a big sigh through lips circled into an O-shape. There was a jumpiness to the way he moved around, which, along with his scruffy waistcoat, misaligned collar and limp bowtie, made up the sort of human that would put any cat ill at ease. His fingers were continually *tap-tap-tapping*, and Grimalkin was convinced he was the type who went about their business far too quickly as if there was a fire around every corner, or a bear careening up the stairwell, or a marauding army of Jacobites about to scale the tenement walls. This behaviour was at odds with Grimalkin's, who, like all Victorian cats, knew a thing or two about taking his time and tending to his appearance properly. It was like being around a jack-in-the-box . . . an awful spring-loaded human who could leap and surprise at any moment and positively ruin a good slumber.

I wish he'd bally-well SLOW DOWN. Such unrestful behaviour!

It didn't help matters that there appeared to be something on the man's mind. Something important.

A thought occurred to Grimalkin. *He cannot see me, but I wonder if he can hear me?* With that, he opened his mouth and let out a gentle, but concerted purr-mew.

Prrrrrp? Prrrrrrrrrrrrr woaw?

But the man did not respond.

Silence briefly filled the space between cat and man as the gentleman took a pipe from his breast pocket. Drumming his fingers, he plucked a tin from a little adjacent table from which he extracted a healthy amount of stringy tobacco and a box of matches. Striking one of the matches, he guided the flame to the two gas lamps that curled out from the mantlepiece like the necks of swans. Blue-yellow flames leaped out from the sconces as the lit match approached, spurting like fiery dragon breath, and reflecting for a moment on the man's forehead.

"Heavens, Archie, man, pull yourself together!" blurted the gentleman to himself, tossing his tobacco box back on the side table. "You're a *publisher*, for God's sake. He should fear *you* if anything. Just be civil. JM Barrie.[2] Humph! So, he's started doing well for himself. Well, who hasn't in this day and age? The whole world's on the make what with motorcars and electric lights and God knows what else! JM Barrie? Why he's just like everybody else! And I need not fear him; you hear that, Archie, ol' bean? You *need not fear him.*" The man

---

[2] JM Barrie in 1909 had already made a name for himself publishing *Quality Street* (1901) and *The Little White Bird* (1902).

fell silent for a moment. Grimalkin scrutinised his brow to see if any secrets of his character lurked there.

Prrrrrpppppppp ... said Grimalkin, this time a little louder. *No, he cannot hear me. For three he stays, for three he strays, for three he plays. I am only meant to observe in this age ... with no poltergeist capabilities, and perhaps no power to roam beyond this flat either. This gentleman and I shall have to get better acquainted.*

Unseen observation felt exciting to Grimalkin: the thrill of the gaze, unthreatened, with the only prospect of pain being that which is emotional, rather than physical; the chance to witness the unvarnished truth of the ages! He wanted to find out what happened and who this JM Barrie character was. Evidently, he was a writer of some sort, though not one Grimalkin had ever heard of during Queen Victoria's reign. There had been piles of books he'd slept on and, occasionally, perused, back in the nineteenth century; but they had all been written by a certain Robert Louis Stevenson, who was preoccupied with lighthouses, or Elizabeth Gaskell, who was obsessed with wizened old clerks and long descriptions of dirty mills that, frankly, made Grimalkin's whiskers droop.

With a moody burst of energy, the man procured a walking cane from underneath the settee, which he used to jab a wooden button, mounted just to the right of the fireplace. On pushing this, a bell chimed down the hall. There followed a padding of feet. And from those feet alone, Grimalkin could tell who was approaching: the mere dance of that noise into his ears made him slow-blink in fondness. Eilidh.

The doorknob turned and in came Eilidh herself, the same boar-bristle brush in her hand, and the same flushed face, like a little rosy moon, under the same white headdress. Unchanged. She smiled and turned to the master.

"Yes, sir? Can I help ye?"

A delicious scent came with her into the room: one of her famous pies was in the oven, known throughout Edinburgh for its exquisite taste. She breathed heavily. It was then Grimalkin noticed the first signs of age: she was a little wider about the shoulders, and her eyes, though still sparkling, had lost their youthful, girlish twinkle. The pompadour hairstyle had gone; instead, her hair was pulled back in a matronly style that Grimalkin suspected offered maximum practicality for her work and nothing else. Her skin had become thicker, too, and those once perfectly pink cheeks had lost some of their porcelain tautness. But Eilidh's hands were perhaps the biggest change – the skin was cracking about the knuckles, which had clearly become arthritic, and the undersides were so red that Grimalkin suspected they must bleed often. Despite this, her fingernails remained scrupulously clean, the progress of years clearly doing nothing to her habit of scrubbing them free of coal dust after each shift. *Oh, Eilidh!* the same sweet maid who found Grimalkin in Thirlestane Lane stables, and tended to him throughout his young life, right up to his dying day in 1902!

Here she was, standing in front of him, as if he could go over and scratch at her stockings for attention, as he had done in the long winter days of the previous century in this very room.

"My, Eilidh, some delightful odours emanating from the kitchen, my girl. What's on the menu?"

"Pork loin with tatties, sir. I had a blether with the butcher down at New Town. He said pork loin was always Master Barrie's favourite, back when he was a student down on Cumberland Street."[3]

A smile came over the man's face. He took his pipe out from between his lips and butted its nub towards Eilidh. "You see, Eilidh, my girl, this is why you are the *best* house-keeper in town. How lucky I am that you were so fond of the bricks and mortar of Marchmont Crescent that you decided to stay here rather than follow your master to New Town. I really would be flummoxed without you. They don't make 'em like you in London, you know!"

"Oh," said Eilidh, blushing, with a half-smile and nod.

"Jolly good, jolly good. Capital stuff. And for pudding?"

"Cranachan, sir, Barrie's favourite as well."

"Splendid, splendid. Well, that'll make for a most agreeable repast, and if your victual cannot impel him to sign with

---

[3] Barrie, the author of *Peter Pan*, lodged at 14 Cumberland Street, Edinburgh, while a student between 1879–1882. His housekeeper truly believed the quality of her pork pies was a pivotal factor in inspiring his genius.

Cavendish & Co, I don't know what will." A solemnness suddenly came over his face. "But *do remember* to await my three rings before starting, yes? Just like we discussed? We want the fellow to be primed and ready to bite. He's a delicate type, so I hear. Lost his brother aged thirteen back in '67 ... Never got over it, apparently."

"Aye, ice skating. Terrible. I remember reading about it in the papers, sir."

"Well, yes, yes, quite. Poor chap. But fortunately for *me* ..." Here the master plucked out his pipe again, pointing its end in Eilidh's direction "... it informed his genius. With a little diddle here and tickle there, that genius could be mine to sell. Oh, and would you bring the script through from my bureau, please, my girl? It's one marked *Peter and Wendy*. Mr Barrie should be here presently."

"Aye, sir."

A mixture of love and aching sadness swilled around Grimalkin's belly like hot milk. Seeing Eilidh had brought home the cruelty of time's unstoppable progress. It's not that she had aged *badly*, but she had aged, as someone in her line of work inevitably would, faster than the likes of Mr Cavendish, whom she served. Time had etched its passing in lines and curves and the loosening of skin. Grimalkin's mind started turning over all the possible events – good and bad – that might have affected Eilidh in the interim years. *Has she met a man who had brought her means? Has she kept free from the mischiefs of pestilence and illness? How old must she be now? Nine and twenty?*

Oh, why must I only live my nine lives going forward? he mused, remembering too that Cat-sìth only afforded him poltergeist powers during his three 'playing' lives. He wanted to leap into Eilidh's arms like Alice in the *Alice in Wonderland* books.[4]

A little while later, Eilidh returned with a clutch of brown papers in her hand. The master took them and flicked through them hurriedly, his eye swivelling over each paragraph in turn, before gathering the pages together and placing them under the settee out of sight. Finally, he rose in a determined fashion, brushed his trouser legs free of invisible dust, tweaked his neckerchief in a nearby mirror, and took out an ivory-handled comb from the top drawer of the bureau. He was getting anxious again, bouncing on the balls of his feet, and puffing little gouts of smoke from his pipe into the air like a tiny steam train.

* * *

This gentleman is playing havoc with my nerves, thought Grimalkin irritably, feeling the man's anxiety seep into him. He decided

---

[4] Written by Lewis Carroll and published in 1865. Among the most popular children's books of the late Victorian period. Grimalkin had witnessed Eilidh reading the Carroll books to his master (Mr Calvert's) nephew in 1889. Grimalkin always despised the portrayal of the Cheshire Cat, however, believing its inane grin to be an unpleasant parody of a cat in a state of majestic repose.

to go and explore the flat, trotting over to the lounge door, which he discovered he could melt through with ease.

Good gracious, and they've meddled with the hall as well I see.

Resplendent with opulent tropical plants, the hall was a much brighter, airier space than Grimalkin recalled from previous years. A spiky plant with large leaves, the likes of which Grimalkin had only ever spied in the natural history books on Mr Calvert's bureau, sat in a handsome china pot glazed with images of lions and tigers prancing against colourful Japanese script. The front door, which had been painted white, now boasted an exquisite stained-glass window above it, depicting a stag in the Highlands, its front leg raised gallantly. At opposite sides of the hall, gas lamps sang out blue and yellow flames from their brass necks.

Grimalkin's ear twitched. Excitable chatter was coming from behind the furthest door. He could recall the room immediately in his mind's eye – it was his late master's bedchamber; the one with the view of the great sycamore tree in the communal garden which was fantastic for bluetit watching. Grimalkin could pick out Eilidh's voice *ooooh*-ing and *ahhhh*-ing alongside another that gabbled in an irritating high pitch, like a bell.

Well, what goes on here, I wonder, thought Grimalkin, sashaying his way through the centre of the door.

Upon entering, he was surprised to find the room in pitch darkness. The shutters had been closed, and all the gas lamps extinguished on the walls.

Suddenly, everything was bathed in a blinding light.

"It is remarkable, truly remarkable!" chimed a lady, hemmed in a tight corset. "And entirely safe! Mr Monteith and his men installed them on Tuesday. Every floorboard was up; it was a veritable *state* I can tell you. Are you ready, Eilidh? Oh, tell me you're ready! Let us do it again. Three, two ..."

On "one", the lady gave two flicks to a little handle mounted on a circular fixing by the door. The room fell dark and light again.

"Ha ha ha! It's positively marvellous, is it not, Eilidh? Eeee-leeecc-trrreee-cccity? Ha ha ha."

My word, she's shrewish and irritating, thought Grimalkin, lowering his ears and stalking over to Eilidh's ankles.

"Aye, yes, ma'am. Very impressive," said Eilidh, trying hard to look interested. "And how long before one must replenish the reserve, ma'am?"

"That's the beauty, Eilidh!" said the woman. "With the new electricity, our lights will never run out. Not now, not tomorrow ... Not ever! And all safe and all clean. You should see Lady Richardson's parlour down in Morningside. A thousand lights twinkling like a West End stage; it feels like broad daylight at eleven o'clock at night!"[5]

---

[5] The excitement for the electric light probably stems from 1909 being the year that the second Electric Lighting Act was introduced. This enabled the Board of Trade to authorise mains electricity to all regions of the country, much to the chagrin of cats like Grimalkin, who often enjoyed singeing their whiskers in candle flames so they twizzled into jaunty spirals. Prior to 1909, the electric light was mainly limited to non-domestic settings, with even wealthy homes like 7/7 Marchmont Crescent continuing to use gas, candles and oil-based energy.

"Saints preserve us," said Eilidh under her breath. "May I have a turn, ma'am?"

"Why of course! You are family, Eilidh, you always will be. And Mr Monteith tells me there is an electricity – um hole ..." At this, she pointed to a little round plate down by the floor, "... in the pantry for your convenience."

Eilidh flicked the light on and off just once, in the humble way of a servant acting under the watchful eye of their employer. "How miraculous."

A moment later a noise came from down the hall – a sharp *tinkle-inkle-inkle-inkle-inkle.*

Fie, the blasted chime of hell!

Grimalkin knew the noise immediately. Marchmont Crescent's pulley doorbell was enough to make any dozing cat leap from their perch. He hated it and its piercing little peal. More than this, unlike the humans, Grimalkin could also tell the character of the person ringing it. His master, if he had forgotten his key, would give three long, slow pulls, giving rise to a long continuous peal like a provincial church calling parishioners to evensong – gallant, important and bold. This ring, however, was snappy and short – just one yank of the brass handle down at the communal door. Grimalkin could tell that the visitor, no doubt this enigmatic Mr Barrie, was in an impetuous, argumentative mood. The coalmen in Victorian times used the same ring, and they were always thus.

Grimalkin glided out into the hall, sheltering behind one of the great china flowerpots, belly to the ground. Eilidh scurried ahead and peeked through the spyhole like a conspiratorial squirrel.

"Aye, that's him," she whispered to herself, as the lady of the house confined herself to her bedchamber. Eilidh tweaked the strings at the back of her headdress and patted the sides of her hair, her big red hands trembling slightly. Grimalkin could almost feel her excitement prickle through the air and into his fur. Carefully, Eilidh unlatched the familiar set of fat bolts that ran down the door frame and pulled it open.

Mr Barrie stood perfectly centred in the door frame, pristine and still like marble. He was a little out of breath. At first sight, the man seemed quite unremarkable: his dress, for the main part, was similar to what the master had been wearing . . . And yet so small and thin was Mr Barrie, that clothes appeared altogether different on him. His dark coat and tails hung loosely on his tiny frame, making him look like a schoolboy dressed in a uniform his mother hoped he'd grow into over the coming term. This was topped off with a brown cravat and white collar, and a thin hand clutching a folded umbrella so tightly you could see the whites of his knuckles. His eyes, though soft, nestled in dark sockets that seemed to possess a wealth of strange pains, and they observed Eilidh with the nervousness of a child about to be rebuked. Was it sorrow there? Mourning? Heartache? Grimalkin couldn't tell. Fortunately, Mr Barrie's protruding ears gave his face an ungainly almost comic aspect, that made him appear unthreatening. This effect was aided by a moustache too large and bushy for his face, which sloped downwards, giving him a hangdog, somewhat basset hound-like jawline.

"I must apologise," said Mr Barrie awkwardly. "Your communal door was ajar. I took the liberty of venturing in."

"Oh, to be sure, of course, Mister B— I mean, sir," gabbled Eilidh, a beam fixed across her features. Grimalkin followed the pair through to the lounge.

"Ah, Mr Barrie, an absolute pleasure," said the master, bouncing to his feet. "Tremendous thanks for gracing me with your company this evening. Do sit, do sit. Um, Eilidh ... Perhaps some port for Mr Barrie?"

Mr Barrie nodded stiffly.

The two men sat down sidelong on the sofa, Barrie still clutching his umbrella.

"Uhm, Eilidh," said the master. "Could you also take Mr Barrie's coat and umbrella? Rather warm in here, but cold as a cast-iron commode outside, ha! You do know they're starting to affix part of Edinburgh to the new electricity grid, Barrie? Have it in the back bedroom already. But months away and we'll all be bathed with the warm glow of the electric light, how wondrous!"

"I've heard it kills you," said Mr Barrie with a frown as he wriggled free of his coat like a butterfly shedding its pupa. He handed it over to Eilidh with a nod.

"Ah, well, yes, yes, of course *that* side of things is still to be addressed." The master shuffled his posterior on the settee and dropped his tone a notch.

39

"Now, I'll get straight on with it, ol' bean," he said. "This *Peter and Wendy* . . . It's capital stuff, old fellow. Truly spiffing. And I believe it'd make a splendid novel following the success of the stage show. It's marvellous. I love all this sibling frolicking; that's what made your play *Quality Street* such a success after all. I'm hugely disappointed I couldn't catch it when it was here at the King's Theatre last month, but there was a backstage fire and they had to refund our tickets.[6] But I'm thinking, Barrie, and forgive me for being a dunderhead about it, old chap, but . . . perhaps we can dial back on some of Peter Pan's magical stuff – all these fairy-tale japes and whatnot – for the American market? Oh, and perhaps make Pan a little more . . . " He made a circle in the air with the end of his pipe. "Savvy. Yes, savvy. A tad less impetuous. All that flying! That worries the public . . . They'll see it as promoting reckless behaviour. Apparently, you see, this is going to be the next big thing . . . " With that, he picked up a slim book from under the coffee table entitled *Die Traumdeutung* by Sigmund Freud.[7]

Grimalkin saw a hunted look come over Barrie's eyes; the sort of wide-eyed stare he could well recall in the eyes of a

---

[6] On 12 July 1909, the King's Theatre narrowly escaped fire. A dropped match backstage was left smouldering overnight. A passer-by raised the alarm in the early hours of the morning.

[7] Later translated into English as *The Interpretation of Dreams* in 1913.

vole or rat whenever he had cornered them in the communal gardens, back in the 1880s.

"Ah, yes," said the master, slapping his legs. "But if you address that, and a few tweaks here and there … Well, I believe Cavendish & Co could make you a jolly good offer on it. A jolly good offer indeed! We'd require lifetime rights, plus a hundred years, naturally. All standard stuff. So! What sort of figure would you deem fair?"

The master took a puff of his pipe in that self-satisfied way of someone who has said their bit and is rather pleased with how it had formed on their lips. Mr Barrie's eyes darted around the room – up to the cornice, and then down to the rug, then over to the picture above the fireplace. An odd gravitas came across his frame. He straightened upright and took in a deep breath, canting his head back slightly as if about to drink from a stream of water.

By Jove, the man's a genius! I can tell! He's a one-in-a-million genius!

"Uuuh, Mr Barrie?" said the master. "Are you quite well, sir? What think you, then?"

Mr Barrie set his chin into his shirt collar, his oversized moustache bristling like a boot brush as his lips moved and tried to find the right words. Eventually he lifted his head, staring the master straight between the eyes.

"Thank you for your kind offer, sir," he said carefully. "The generosities dealt towards my early works by yourself have always been gratefully received, in spite of the occasional …

disconnect of vision." He shifted somewhat uncomfortably on the settee, his bony knees clamped firmly together. "You see, I wouldn't want to alter Peter Pan too much. That recklessness ... it's a mainstay of his character, Cavendish. It is his superpower, his lance; it's what ensures his beguiling hold on others. I feel, as others do, that it bespeaks great intelligence."

Yes, you tell him, sir! thought Grimalkin, leaping up onto the sofa to better hear Mr Barrie's comments, which sometimes got lost amid the clink and scuffle of Eilidh preparing the glasses in the kitchen.

"And I do not wish to dilute or tamper with these traits, sir. Not for America, not for Britain ... Not for any person for that matter. Peter Pan will remain as he is."

There was a silence as the master placed his pipe on the table. He cleared his throat, as a loudening tinkle came from down the hallway as Eilidh neared with a tray of port glasses.

"Ah, well ... At least tell me you'll think about it, ol' bean? Why, I was about to table one thousand guineas?"

Mr Barrie looked up, shocked.

"Hurrrumph ... That got your attention, didn't it, ha!"

"As I say ... " stuttered Barrie.

"Fifteen hundred?"

"Sir ... "

"Oh, come on!" The master slammed down his pipe, just as Eilidh entered the living room. Sensing the awkwardness, she faltered at the threshold, the port tumblers jingling on a silver tray. Taking a breath, she resumed walking slowly into the room, extending a glass towards Mr Barrie, who took it in his hand before downing it in one huge gulp, his eyes gummed shut and his face pinched with its fragrant heat.

He placed the tumbler down on the table with a clang.

"Mr Cavendish, *Peter and Wendy* is not for sale."[8]

Grimalkin's Observations

Decoration: Lots of indoor flowers and fancy china pots.

Humans: Mr Cavendish. A publisher. Needs to calm his nerves.

Technology: The electric light.

Monarch: King Edward VII.

---

[8] Barrie left Marchmont Crescent shortly after the exchange and never met with the publisher Archie Cavendish again. The novel rights of *Peter Pan* were eventually bought by Hodder & Stoughton in 1911. In 1929, Barrie bequeathed the rights of *Peter Pan* to Great Ormond Street Hospital in London. The hospital still earns royalties for every Peter and Wendy-related film, book or play produced or shown to this day.

Second Haunting,
October 1935

I still remember him as I pass through the street
which saw events worthy of history
but not worth remembering.

– from "On a Stray Cat" by Eugenio Montale

"MY DARLING ALEC DOES NOT know his talents. That's the *problem*, Abigail."

"Uh-huh. It's the quiet types. They get us with their glances and sweet nothings, then turn us half mad. It's a swizz."

Grimalkin awoke with a start. Both his ears had pivoted back and his eyes were wide in the manner of all cats when they've been awoken by a sudden noise.

My golly, I feel rum this morning. Pure rum and ribald. This time travel was all a mistake, a terrible mistake.

He shook his head as if to free himself from the ache that nested there. Cat-sìth had explained that he'd sleep once one haunting was completed, but he never mentioned feeling pained about the head when he awoke into the next. And the incessant human chatter that was emanating from somewhere wasn't helping.

Eventually, he found the strength to fully open his eyes. The room stretched into focus.

He was in the back bedroom at Marchmont Crescent again; the same room in which Eilidh and the woman with the shrill voice had been trying out the new electric bulb. Light was printing bright triangles on the wallpaper, which was patterned in a repeating sequence of red and blue diamonds. A single curtain hung from above the window frame, parted by its waist with a fat scarlet cord, and from beyond the window there came the echoey chitter of a jackdaw in the trees.

Grimalkin was sitting on what appeared to be an ornate vanity table that was perfectly level with the sill of the window. He stared out at the great sycamore in the garden, a sudden knot of nostalgia in his belly. Its leaves had turned auburn and were flaking off in clutches as a rough wind beat around them.

It must be autumn. I could do with a jaunt in that air to purge this foul head. Why can't a cat's course through time be made easy, without all this damnation and humbug . . .

"Oh, Abigail, how I wish he'd command the respect he deserves!" came one of the voices, impetuously.

Two women sat facing each other at either side of the fireplace. The one that had awoken Grimalkin from his time-slumber spoke with an Irish accent and had little black ringleted curls at the top of her head which bounced whenever she spoke. She reminded Grimalkin of Mrs Cavendish from 1909, but her energy was more endearing ... More infectious and interesting to behold. She sat at the edge of her seat, brushing the hem of her skirt as she spoke to a second lady.

This second woman, who sat at a dressing table the opposite side of the fireplace, was unlike any human Grimalkin had ever beheld. She spoke in fitful bursts, with long r's and vowel sounds that made Grimalkin feel she must be from the furthest reaches of the Empire. In contrast to this, her every movement was luxuriant and slow like treacle being squeezed through muslin. What's more, Grimalkin found himself transfixed by her bold, elegant beauty. Her hair was coal-black and clung to her head like a cap, rather unlike anything he had ever beheld on human or beast. Around her cheeks, two little fronds of hair pointed forwards, as if pulled by an invisible string, and where it swept across her temples, it rippled, like the waves of the sea. It was all held in place by a thin, gem-encrusted headband into which a huge spray of maroon feathers had been speared. Her skin was wax-doll white, with just a little red spattering here and there where sunlight caught a spot of blusher powder that had not yet been fully rubbed in. She was applying a dark line about her eyes with a small brush, and something about her perfectly meticulous hand movements made Grimalkin's claws contract. Everything about her was slow and steady like the gentle, unerring revolving of a gramophone's turntable. In opposition, the small bouncy woman who sat facing her spoke in a fretful Irish accent, her hair springing about her cheeks.

And as for the room ... It could not have appeared more different to when Grimalkin last saw it in 1902. It was positively exploding with sharp lines! There were sharp lines on a blue crystal vessel standing on a dressing table beside the mantlepiece. The chair to the left of the fire hearth that the Irish lady was perched on had a ridged back that reminded Grimalkin of Eilidh's old cleaning rack. Over on the far wall hung an eye-catching mirror, cut into the shape of a gemstone, that reflected back a miniaturised version of the room; and on the floor, leaning up against the walls as if they had just been delivered, rested an array of artworks, each housed in a gilt-edged frame. So vibrant and erratic were the coloured lines and blobs and cubes on these canvases that Grimalkin could hardly decipher what it was he was meant to be looking at.

"And now, he's playing it down," continued the Irish woman, a redness coming to her cheeks. "Says we don't have the money or time to devote to research. But I saw with my own eyes, dear Abigail ... it killed bacteria *inside* the body."

"Sounds kinda kooky, Sarah, but I take your word, doll," said the elegant lady, Abigail, in a low, staccatoed kind of voice. Grimalkin studied her as she leaned in towards the mirror to apply a perfect line of red lipstick, her eyes fixed on her mouth's reflection like a poacher staring through crosshairs. "The world has little time for quiet guys, honey. My youngest brother is going the same way, just like my dad ... hoi-polloing and bumping gums with the British royalty. He was down at King George V's jubilee back in May, toadying with that ... Oh, what's he called ... "

"Duke of Gloucester ... " said Sarah.

"No ... The heir to the throne, the pasty fella ... Looks like a tyrant ... Wallis Simpson's clinger on."

"Oh, Prince Edward!"

"Yeah, that's the one. Hell knows what Wallis sees in him. A loada saps, the lot of them."

Fie, wash your mouth out! Grimalkin flinched with a sudden onset of anger. *That's no way to speak of our incumbent king. Whoever he is, he'll no doubt be good and noble and highly able ...*

"I don't know what they see in all those pug dogs," said Sarah.

Curse the king! thought Grimalkin. *What kind of self-respecting king owns a pug as a companion? The sooner he abdicates, the better!*

"But hey, that's not the real world," continued Abigail, snapping shut a jewel-encrusted make-up box, and swivelled on her chair to face the Irish woman. "The *real* world is people like you and your genius husband. Your Alec ... "

"You as well, Abigail," said Sarah a little fawningly. "You do your best to live a normal life."

"Ha! Me? A normal life? There's no part of a Rockefeller's existence that is remotely normal, doll," chanted Abigail. "Yeah, so the Depression affects us a bit, but so what? It hardly makes us any closer to the Kentucky farmer trying to get a shoot to grow in his dusty soil, or a Broadway shoeshine boy. A proud American, yes. A believer in freedom and the Dream, maybe. But, normal? Uh-uh."

"But you could be like the rest of your family," said Sarah. "And yet you choose to do charity work and travel the world for good causes."

"I guess," Abigail replied with a sigh. "The least I can do. Christ, there's gotta be someone to let the odd dime slip from that stinking gold mountain. And it's not like I live like a pauper. I sailed over here on the *Queen Mary* . . ."

"Is that the new one? My, what's it like?"

"Meeeh, kinda snazzy, I guess. But it's like all those British liners. It looks the part but the staff are lousy nincompoops. They lost half my artwork in the holds. Only just received it back. No booze one evening, only dog soup, because they smashed the red-wine crate. But hey, they didn't strike an iceberg and we arrived in the right country, so for the Brits I guess that's a win, right?"

A silence fell as Sarah's eyes jumped admiringly about the room's luscious appointments and furniture. Grimalkin found himself following suit. Then it suddenly hit him: something must be behind all this sharp-edged splendour and bold design. All these alarming geometric shapes and protrusions . . . They smacked of a world wanting to forget; to start afresh.

What on earth has happened in these intervening years? It feels so recent that I observed Mr Barrie on the settee in 1909 . . . A trifling six and twenty years ago. But something momentous must have come to pass to prompt all these spiky styles and radical shapes? The Victorian living chamber is truly dead and buried.

Sarah's brooding eyes came to rest on a newspaper that lay folded at the foot of the bedspread. "Is this the thing they're building in New York?" She gathered the folded pages in her hands. Grimalkin jumped onto the bedspread to catch the headline: *New Rockefeller Skyscraper to Open in Months.*[1]

"Oh yeah, that's one of Daddy's," said Abigail. "A real butter and egg project. He's still bummed out his buildings aren't as tall as the Chrysler so he's compensating by building a ton of them. Way over budget. All stupid, if you ask me." She twirled the crystal stopper in a bottle of Chanel No 5. "Got a telegram last night saying it'd open Tuesday morning."

Sarah examined the front page up and down, circling her finger and thumb together in idle amazement. "Well, I think it's . . . " She paused, reconsidering her words. "If I had to say anything about it, I'd say it's . . . "

"Yeah, damn ugly, right?"

The two of them began to giggle. "It's like some awful grey brick. That's what you were thinking too, right?"

And that was when it happened.

---

[1] The International Building (45 Rockefeller Plaza) was completed in 1935.

By Jove, what are the chances? The ring!

If a thousand universes replayed the same moment between the same women, in the same age, over and over, never again would chance permit the fluke set of bounces and rolls to repeat themselves in quite the same way. It was like peeking through a gap in time; the fissures that splice our world and multiple other universes. As Abigail distracted herself in laughter, a large, pink-gemmed ring dropped off the edge of the dressing table, before bouncing along the floor and disappearing. From what Grimalkin could tell, it had fallen down a gap in the floorboards. It was a particular quirk of this room that Grimalkin knew well, as a hand basin had once stood there just above, back in the 1890s. Mr Calvert had had it removed when he sought to make space in which to store his ever-increasing collection of model steam trains. This little hole in the loose floorboard was all that remained.

My, I recall lapping from that sink, thought Grimalkin, mooching over and standing in the space the sink once occupied. *Never did dog soup taste as snazzy as it did from that leaky faucet. Gosh, I'm thinking in the tongue of the age! Is it this easy to wingding among the gold diggers?*

Ever since, throughout the remainder of his life as a sentient being, Grimalkin recalled that hole always letting in an unpleasant draught, despite Eilidh's best efforts to stuff it with newspaper and cheesecloth. On winter evenings, when the fire had begun to dwindle in the grate, Grimalkin would become acutely aware of this pesky little gap, defiantly giving access to the biting air that whipped off the Pentland Hills. In the end, he had stopped sleeping there altogether, for it is better for a cat to sleep soundly and enduringly than to awake from the perfect slumber owing to a disagreeable change in atmosphere.

*   *   *

Both women continued to talk unawares. Still slightly disbelieving of his newfound invisibility, Grimalkin skirted the corner of the room to peer down the hole where the ring had fallen. A cat's vision is sharper than any human's, but even with his excellent sight, Grimalkin could see nothing down the hole but blackness.

Why, if they hadn't been so careless they could have stopped it rolling asunder. They'll never find it down there.

The laughter between the ladies had eased the slightly stiff atmosphere, and Sarah was now speaking freely with large waves of the hands.

"Just *how much* is our age going to leave to the imagination?" said Sarah. "Soon everything will be injected into our heads . . . "

"By one of my daddy's bootlegging Wall Street tycoons," said Abigail, wryly. "Anyway," she barked, a serious look coming over her face. She closed a drawer on her make-up table before pirouetting round on her chair to face Sarah. "You were saying about your feller Alec discovering something . . . I wanna know about it. Tell me more . . . "

"Oh, aye," said Sarah, with a roll of the eyes. "'I've discovered something, and I think it could change the world,' he tells me in that darling soft way of his. Such a gentle man, my Alec. Anyway, we settled down to supper and he started talking about this mould growing in his lab. Apparently, when we came back from holiday, some old dishes had been piled up in the sink there ... "

"Where's his lab?" chimed in Abigail.

"St Mary's Medical School, near Paddington."

"Huh, yeah, I've heard of Pe-dding-ton. Go on ... "

"Well, apparently this was a really special kind of mould that had gathered on the old plates. It must've come from the surrounding air, he thinks. He's named it 'penicillin' ... Said it could act like an antiseptic, but one that works *inside* the body, rather than on the skin ... "

"Sounds wacky," said Abigail, her elegant hand reaching for a long cigarette holder on the bedside table. "Didn't they try that in the war and find it poisonous?"

So there has been a war, thought Grimalkin with a deep pang. *Oh, capricious fate, make it so that Eilidh has not succumbed to this wretched event. If she has, I don't believe I would have the strength to continue this odyssey through time.*

Abigail swivelled back again to face Sarah, pulling a little silver wisp of cigarette smoke through the air. Grimalkin now saw her face closer than he'd seen it before, her eyes deep and dark and her skin perfectly smooth and white like a doll's.

"That's what I thought," continued Sarah. "I mentioned the war too. However, penicillin is completely harmless. He's on to something, I can sense it. The problem we have is that he needs the funding and the workforce to bring his discovery to light. No one was interested in his paper when he delivered it, and oh, it breaks my heart. And now two years have passed and he's back in the garden every afternoon, gathering leaves for bonfires, like nothing has happened. And all I can think about is how my darling Alec is harbouring this great epic secret . . . This *thing* that could cure disease, end the suffering of millions. But he's too meek . . . Too shy and self-deprecating to push for what's needed. But I know my Alec, my darling Ayrshire lad! I have never forgotten the look he gave me that day; the flash of sheer excitement behind his eyes . . ."

"Humph," said Abigail. There was a pause as she toyed with the pin on an emerald brooch before pinning it to her blouse. "You know what, I like the sound of your fella. How about we go to the lounge before we head out and you tell me what he needs. Get that maid with the unpronounceable name to fix us some cocktails. What is her name, it's like Seltic . . . or Celtic, right? Eee-leeeee?"

She lives! My Eilidh outlived the conflict and is here! Grimalkin's heart settled, his eyes dropping with relief.

Sarah giggled. "Oh, it is pronounced 'ayyy-leee' in Scotland."

"Well, why all the unnecessary letters? Is it just to throw off foreigners like me? Get us to stand out like nincompoops?"

55

The pair of them rose and headed to the hallway. Grimalkin noticed Abigail falter as she neared the door. Suddenly, in that way of hers, she spun around to face the room again, her slender white fingers feeling the index finger of her left hand. "Say, did you see what I did with that damned ring?"

"The gold one?"

"No, the pink diamond. It was here somewhere, I swear it. Hey, can you see it under that closet?" She kneeled, looking under the chairs and dressing table. "Humph, something about this country is putting my brain in a funk. I'm losing stuff left, right and centre. I blame the boiled sheep guts ... "

Sarah laughed politely.

"Humph, it'll show up. Anyway."

A strong scent of rosy perfume followed in the women's wake as they sashayed out into the hall. It almost made Grimalkin's eyes water. He trotted after them intently, tail high with excitement, desperate to catch a glimpse of Eilidh.

"Hey, you there, missy!" shouted Abigail. "Say, could you fix us a couple of Scotches, on the ice, say in ten minutes' time?"

Abigail had come to a stop just beside the stained-glass window above the front door depicting the Highland stag, its flank sparkling and red with the evening sunlight that poured through from the tenement stairway cupola. There, standing just beneath it with red cheeks and broad shoulders, the sweet smell of beeswax polish exuding around her like a halo, was Eilidh. She had been tending a potted plant that stood beside the front door, pulling out its dead and browning fronds. *She's here. She has walked this earth all this time, her heart beating every day!*

Seeing Eilidh continuing her work as humbly and diligently as ever gave Grimalkin a confusing mix of feelings. On the one hand, he was sad that she hadn't managed to rise above her station and secure some means via a well-bred gentleman or vaulted social standing. On the other hand, he was happy to see her tall and healthy in front of him, her skin flushed and taut, and her ox-like form stoic against the passing of years. Her hair, once coal-black, was a little wiry now and flecked with grey, and the pinny – still with its trademark array of small splodges and stains – seemed to be pulled uncomfortably tight around her waist and shoulders.

Without thinking, Grimalkin made straight for her ankles, his side poised to rub along her stockings.

But he glided straight through her.

Oh, damnation, this is downright wicked. Must I wait till my poltergeist lives before I am able to sense the flesh?

Yet he could still smell her.

Taking a long in-breath, all Eilidh's smells came rushing into Grimalkin's nostrils all at once. A human would no doubt have smelled beeswax polish on her and nothing else; but a cat's nose is far more sensitive. In fact, Grimalkin could smell such a constellation of fragrances dancing underneath the trademark beeswax aroma that he was able to tell, in an instant, that her household chores, and habits and recipes, had remained largely unchanged with time. There was the earthy, starchy scent of her hands as she scraped the potato peels into the compost in the communal garden. There was the waxen whiff of dish soap that travelled up her arms when she scrubbed pie dishes in the scullery sink. Beneath this was the spicy tang of paraffin, and the thick heady aroma of coal dust and polish that combined indistinguishably with the smell of metalwork. And then of course the cooking – the famous suet pudding recipe still hung with mouth-watering nearness about her apron. It all combined to make a scent that was so unmistakably Eilidh that it instantly transported Grimalkin back to kittenhood, and Thirlestane Lane in 1887, when he, a mewling kitten, had been scooped up by a seven-year-old Eilidh when she was little more than an apprentice char girl still in the care of her mother.

"Certainly, ma'am," said Eilidh, as the two ladies proceeded into the lounge. Grimalkin mewed through the empty air in long sonorous pitiful cries. Anything. If he could get as much as a glance from Eilidh, it would make him feel less lonely, and more connected to this new world.

But it was no use. Eilidh stood as if behind a wall of glass – hearing nothing, seeing nothing, smelling nothing.

No, there's something amiss . . . thought Grimalkin, eyeing Eilidh's shoulders again, which struck him as being sloped and a little rounded. *Something is wrong . . .*

There seemed on Eilidh the weight of an invisible burden. It was hard to describe but a cat's sense for hidden ills is acute and rarely misjudged. Something more subtle was gnawing at Eilidh's spirit. Grimalkin trotted ahead of her down the hall so that he might look back and see her face. He caught a glimpse just as she turned to enter the box room.[2] *Yes, there! Why had the light disappeared from behind her eyes?*

Alone in the hall, the two ladies installed in the lounge, Eilidh's smile had vanished like breath on cold glass. On closer inspection, her cheeks were flecked with yellow blotches, like tallow, and her eyes seemed watery and empty of sparkle.

Keeping beside Eilidh's heel, Grimalkin entered the box room. There he immediately discovered the probable source of Eilidh's unhappiness. The box room had always been the master's bureau in Victorian times – a good enough space to pen a letter in, but given its lack of windows and absence of any fire grate, it was no fit space to reside in. But here in 1935, much to Grimalkin's horror, it had been repurposed into Eilidh's bedroom and store cupboard combined.

Heavens above, there is scarce space in here to swing me by the tail. Grimalkin's thoughts tumbled over themselves. *Where does one sleep? Where does one find repose? Where are the pictures on the wall or the view of the out-of-doors to fix the soul?*

---

[2] In the UK, a box room is a very small room often used as a spare bedroom or large cupboard. In Edinburgh flats, they're famous for housing actors working the Festival Fringe, or students subletting short-term to their friends under the beady-eyed watch of landlords.

59

Bottles and jars of differing colours piled high, forming precarious towers. These spaces were unpleasantly small for a human, but they were tantalising for any cat: so many places to hide ... so many items to knock or spill. Grimalkin's eyes hungered across the array of strange bottles with large colourful logos that looked much more eye-catching than any labels he'd seen in the nineteenth century. There was Dustbane Sweeping Compound in an orange-coloured cylinder, which was opened with a spoon on the top. Then there was Fiebing's Saddle Soap and Carters Borax Soap, and Brasso piled high in a pyramid on a shelf above the bed's headboard, its red, white and blue logo blasting its presence alarmingly into the room. A cushion beater hung from a nail next to a tin bath that was so huge Eilidh had to draw in her breath and inch past it sideways in order to enter the room.

My, the back-scritcher! She still has the back-scritcher!

Hanging from a brass hook, oval and prickly like a little hedgehog, was Eilidh's scrubbing brush. Its bristles were comprised of thick, red boar's hair that was sharp to the paw and made an almighty *cr-sssssh cr-sssssh* when sweeping against any surface. Alongside was its partner in crime, the dustpan, with its wide-mouthed metal tongue, lip bent with wear, and brass nameplate bearing Eilidh's family name "MacNeil" faded from all the dust. She had inherited it from her mother, and it had clearly been well-made as it had little carvings around the base of the handle. Seeing it hanging there took Grimalkin right back to his first life, more so perhaps than anything else he'd seen at Marchmont Crescent, excepting Eilidh herself. It brought to mind one of his earliest memories: in it, he was rubbing his back along the brush's ribbed handle to relieve an itch while just beyond the bay window, snowflakes fell through the streetlamp's glow. *That must have been, what . . . Christmas 1889, Grimalkin? No later!* Often, when doing this, he would send the brush clattering to the floor, much to the chagrin of Eilidh's mother, who would scold him for waking up Mr Calvert in the early hours.

But Eilidh herself would never scold him. Instead, as her mother set the fire, she would take the brush and run its handle up and down Grimalkin's back, setting him into drooling ecstasy. As a result, it was, and always would be for him, "the back-scritcher".

Poor Eilidh. To repose and slumber among this pell-mell must be torturous, thought Grimalkin, his whiskers brushing the myriad items as he snaked in and out of them along the floor.

As Grimalkin's eyes adjusted, he gradually began to discern Eilidh's personal items among the overwhelming clutter of tins, jars and objects. A small wrought-iron bed lay butted up to the far wall, beside which stood a puny chest of drawers. The chest of drawers was so small as to be almost doll-sized. *I couldn't curl up in one of those drawers,* Grimalkin found himself thinking as Eilidh walked ahead of him, taking up a large pile of newly laundered bedsheets and laying them at the foot of her bed.

With a sigh, she sat on the counterpane, loosening the back of her pinny. A lamp squatted on a side table, more a plinth than a bedside table, which was sending out a fizzing light, that Grimalkin could only assume was being powered by this newly ubiquitous "electricity". As Eilidh folded her pinny to her side, Grimalkin noticed a photograph. It was scarcely bigger than a postage stamp, and bore the image of a broad-shouldered handsome man, with a carefree smile and definite twinkle in his eye.

A husband?

Grimalkin leaped upon the bed, which felt hard and unyielding beneath his paws.

My . . . gosh!

On closer inspection, the man in the frame was barely an adult, but a young boy on the turn into adulthood. He was standing upon a large stretch of parkland next to a little placard that read "Middle Meadow Walk". It was difficult to tell his age, for he had one of those youthful smooth faces and dimpled smiles that could belie a much older age, but his army uniform, complete with belt and knee-high boots, suggested he must at least be of military age.

"God help me."

Grimalkin's ears twitched. Eilidh had begun gently crying. A large cloudy tear had beaded just under one of her eyes, and her chest was trembling. With shaking hands, she reached up to the neckline of her dress and pulled out a large chain and crucifix which she had concealed and began clutching it.

She exhaled in puffs, clearly trying to contain the sob within herself for fear she'd be heard by the others in the flat. The scene was almost too painful for Grimalkin to behold. *No one should suffer this pain,* considered Grimalkin. *Not least of all Eilidh, the finest and kindest of all humans.*

Instinctively, Grimalkin tried to purr and rub himself against Eilidh's dress again, but it simply gave way. Several minutes passed as Eilidh brushed down her apron and organised a series of brooms and brushes that lay piled up at the foot of the bed, their sticks projecting into the air like a row of skittles. Eventually, she extracted a tatty book from her bedside table. Grimalkin recognised it immediately as her diary; the very same leather-bound collection of scruffy pages and notes into which she had journalled her thoughts when Grimalkin was still living. With a sigh, she leaned down to pat the floor for a pencil which had rolled into the dusty shadows. Then, wiping a tear and composing herself again, she opened the leather journal and began to write, pausing here and there to wipe another tear.

Briiing! The servants' bell sent out a long peal. Eilidh jumped, letting the pencil slip.

"Ocht, the cocktails!" she whispered to herself, pulling a mirror from her drawer and adjusting her hair.

As Eilidh bustled out of the box room door, Grimalkin found himself looking back at the open diary. He had never read Eilidh's diary in the past, though he had taken a peek at his late master's, who had detailed what he referred to as "My

Travails with Opium and Liquor". He knew the humans guarded their diary thoughts jealously, but something about Eilidh's behaviour, along with this room and the bedside photograph, was sending questions spinning round Grimalkin's head that were too loud to ignore. He simply had to find out what heartache had befallen Eilidh in the years leading to 1935.

He pawed his way across the bed and positioned himself square in front of the leather diary, which lay open with the pencil nestled in the crease of the spine. As the *clink* of cocktail glasses being arranged echoed down the hall, Grimalkin started to read ...

4 October 1935

Alfie, my blessed wee scone! I dreamed of you again last night. It was 1914 again and I was pelting up the Mile to the City Chambers to stop you conscripting. But no sooner had I passed the Tron Kirk than Auld Nick himself grabbed me and pulled me down Bell's Wynd.[3] I scratched and screamed, but by the time I freed myself, it was too late. The conscription clerk said you had boarded the train at Waverley with

---

[3] "Auld Nick", a colloquial term for the Devil in Scotland until the mid-twentieth century. Bell's Wynd is reputedly the most haunted close in Edinburgh and once home to the murderous Mr Guthrie, who, in the eighteenth century, allegedly killed his wife upon discovering her in the arms of a lover.

the other boys. You were already hurtling towards the Somme, Alfie! And I couldn't stop you!

Remember how you had cut the grass at the back of Nana's the night before you left? Had you known, darling Alfie? Had the Devil visited you as well? Had he made you sick to the blood before you even left our shores?

Keep close the angels, darling boy.

They're talking of another war. Germany again, and an evil man called Hitler. And I am still at Marchmont Crescent, just like I was during the last war that took you. And still trying to scrape five shillings a week to get a place of my own. Oh, imagine a pretty little cottage, somewhere like Glenisla Gardens, can you imagine, Alfie!

Sometimes I half hope there is another war. And a bomb. A bomb that ends the pain and brings me back to you, my sweet boy.

There's a famous lady living here. From the richest family on earth, they say. More wealth than even Andrew Carnegie and all his steel . . . [4] *The family has a skyscraper named after them in New York. She may be rich as Croesus but Ol Tam who reads the papers down at Lauder Road says she is the kindest and most generous of her family. She brought this Irish lady back to Marchmont Crescent last night and I overheard*

---

[4] Andrew Carnegie was once the richest man in Scotland. He died in 1919 after giving away all his wealth.

them talking. Apparently, the Irish lady's husband has discovered a special mould that can kill germs in the bloodstream . . . The same germs that had you poisoned in that bleak Somme field. Oh, darling boy, I cannot imagine. They tell me they held you close as you died. Tell me that is true? I hope you felt warm. Oh, give me a sign, Alfie . . . Tell me you felt warm?

There's a fleet of motorcars lined up on the street below. Gleaming like a still loch on a spring morning, so they are. Clarinda at number 60/2 said that one of them even has a radiogram inside it, think of that. You loved unscrewing and fixing radiograms. A little genius you were . . . Destined to work at the Observatory or the University, I would wager. If the devil war hadn't taken you.

The Rockefeller lady has me sending telegrams. You should see the money she gives me! Thick, crisp wads. Notes upon notes upon notes. The postmaster in Morningside thinks me a thief, I am sure of it. Tomorrow I'm to help clean one of the motorcars . . . Oh, the motorcars, Alfie. Did I mention them? You would love their gleaming dials!

I am tired, dear boy. Tired and teary from this reminiscing. I crave companionship . . . Someone to hug as I fall asleep. That little cat. Grimalkin, remember him? Oh, how I loved that wee puss! There was such a curious look in his eyes . . . Like he had been here before and knew what was about to happen. But the sweetest nature . . . Never a scratch or a hiss from him, just all love and . . .

At this point, the diary stopped. Grimalkin's eyes, which had been racing along with the text, fell still. A feeling of power-lessness came over him, much like he felt when being able to see Eilidh but not have her see him back. A deep sadness washed over him, but he knew this feeling was nothing to what Eilidh must be feeling, day in day out . . . To lose a child; to outlive your own baby and have no one to speak to about it; nothing but the pages of a diary.

The years she must have lived in this way, mused Grimalkin, feeling grief on Eilidh's behalf. *The torture we put ourselves through in order to sate our curiosities! Cat-sìth, you charlatan! You might have known my experience would be thus.*

From in the hall there came the familiar sound of the great front door lock turning. Grimalkin peeked round the door frame of the box room; Eilidh was heading into the stairwell, an ashtray in her hand to be emptied in the communal garden and an empty icebox in the other. As she moved off into the grand atrium with its curling stairways above and below, Grimalkin felt an urge to trot after her.

Eilidh's footsteps echoed, gradually getting quieter as they reached the tenement basement. Grimalkin approached the threshold, sniffing the green and white wall tiles, some of which had cracked in the intervening years or become thickly rinded with dirt. All cats become mischievous when they spy a door left ajar, and Grimalkin had an overwhelming urge to bolt out after Eilidh into the chill air of Edinburgh; to run free in the hope he could escape all the knowledge he had just learned in the same way a cat feels they can outrun a bit of thistle bud stubbornly attached to the side of their leg. Suddenly, he found himself charging at the front door, but no sooner had he crossed the door's threshold and slipped under the stained-glass stag than his passage was dramatically stopped. It was as if he had run into a wall ... A wall that could neither be seen nor felt.

Incredulous, he drew back, his fur spiked up and his mouth wrinkled into a hiss which rolled off his tongue for no one to hear. *What the blazes? Why cannot I proceed?*

And then he remembered: the law that underpinned all cats' lives, as retold to him by Cat-sìth.

For three he stayed . . .

The great outdoors of future Edinburgh was barred. For now.

* * *

Back in the living room, the cocktails were already having their effect. Abigail Rockefeller was reclining easily on a chaise longue while the Irish lady, Sarah, was perched a little more stiffly on a peculiar bulbous-looking chair, with a fan-like back of ribbed leather. In Sarah's hand was a long pole that reminded Grimalkin of a candlestick, from which a twisted wire trailed across the floor. The streetlight had clicked on outside, sending in yellow light, which only served to emphasise the opulence of the many artworks that lay stacked in huge gilt frames.

"Jeez, Sarah, don't yell into the thing. You just speak normally. Hold it a little further. Has the operator connected you yet? Wait, give it here . . . "

Abigail picked up the device, which crackled, making Grimalkin suddenly wide-eyed and skittish.

"Okay, so when this happens, you give this a few taps," said Abigail, prodding a little armature. "Here, that's it. Yup. Hey, operator, you there, ma'am?" She placed a little trumpet against her ear. "Now, Sarah, what's that number, 4-2-9-3? Great. *Operator, we want Edinboro, 4-2-9-3 . . .* There." She thrust the device in Sarah's direction, who took it, eyeing it nervously as if it might sprout feet and leap into her face.

"Hello, yes," Sarah intoned softly. "Hello, Mary, can you hear me? Saints preserve! Marvellous, kindly tell Alec I'm to stay another night with Miss Rockefeller at Marchmont Crescent. Ha, how extraordinary!"

And there it is, thought Grimalkin cynically. *They just cannot get enough, can they. First Marconi and semaphore . . . then the radiogram. But still that is not sufficient for them. They must attach candlesticks to the electric lines and communicate down those as well. Why, in time they'll all have a personal telephonic system glued to them and won't ever need to look each other in the eye!*

Grimalkin trotted over to the candlestick, which Sarah had replaced on a side table next to a rather ostentatious statuette of a woman mid-dance. The ear cone now sat on the hinge and reminded him of his late master's father – a real moth-eaten old Victorian – who only ever attended Marchmont Crescent at Christmas and Easter with a large ear trumpet to aid his deafness. Grimalkin sniffed it and was surprised to discover it had a fishy aroma,[5] prompting him to give it a lick. This last decision was a wrongful one, for no sooner had he licked the ear trumpet than he found himself gagging in the kind of pathetic cat fashion that would have been highly embarrassing had anyone actually seen him do it.

"Hey, sit down," said Abigail. Grimalkin watched as she picked up a cigarette case from a side table on which stood a lamp frilled with glass beads around its lampshade. "So I wanna help out your Alec. I think we can make his bug-killing thing work."

Sarah's face turned suddenly serious, her mouth falling slowly agape.

"That Australian guy you mentioned is working on Alec's discovery. Does he go by the name of Florey by any chance?"

"I . . . I think he might . . ." faltered Sarah, her eyes fixed on Abigail like a dog awaiting the next movement of a stick.

"You see my daddy has this fund I'm now in charge of," said Abigail, placing the cigarette in another of the long holders and setting it alight. "It's called the Rockefeller Foundation.

---

[5] In all likelihood Bakelite, an early synthetic plastic, invented in 1907 and used throughout the early half of the twentieth century.

I'm pretty damn sure we've funded Florey to work on microbes and all of that." She said "microbes" with a sweep of her slender fingers through the air, a ribbon of cigarette smoke following behind, in a way that would seem dismissive were it not for the strange gravitas and importance she lent every one of her words. "There's also this other guy I have my eye on. A genius, I'm sure of it. Just come in from Germany, I hear, because you cannot be a Jew there now because of this maniacal Hitler. Say we get the men together – pool all that talent. There's power in numbers. And I'll head up the money – don't think of the price. I'll get it all covered. And hopefully, together, these great men can help get this penicillin thing off the ground ... "

"Would ... I mean," Sarah faltered. "It would take thousands, Abigail ... To run the experiments, to produce it at volume, to distribute and to test and ... "

"Hey!" barked Abigail. "I said I'll cover it already. That's what I do, I'm a philanthropist. That's the *point* of me, doll. I help people get where they need to be because I'm rich. It's either that or I drink myself into a gin-soaked stupor on a superyacht in the Caribbean. And I don't like boats, so ... *God damn*, where is that Eelee maid? Can someone get her to shake a leg?"

She jabbed a button that had been wired up to the side table next to the settee, sending the little glass drops around the nearby lampshade jingling furiously.

"I suppose there's power in numbers," said Sarah, who Grimalkin noticed was clearly attempting to contain her excitement.

71

"Sure, there is. I'll speak to my man Hopkins and get all of them together for dinner. And I'll get plenty of drinks in. I hear your quiet Scottish men don't talk to each other unless there's lots of whisky present. We can't have them staring at each other like nincompoops. And then, when the time comes, I'll foot the bill. Tell your Alec to hold tight. We'll make it happen."

At that moment there was a knock at the door, and Eilidh entered wearing her best smile. Grimalkin had noticed her back had straightened and she was moving in that forced skittish way of someone trying to appear more in control and jolly than they were really feeling.

"Drinks, Miss Rockefeller," she said, curtseying and placing the silver tray of bright pink cocktails on the coffee table.

"Say!" exclaimed Abigail. "I like you, Miss Eylee ... And you're cute as a bug's ear but that hair's doing you no favours, doll. How about you go treat yourself. What's that big hotel in the centre of town you have here ..."

"Err ... " Eilidh stared, a frown ruching above her eyes. "The big hotel, ma'am? Well, there's the Caledonian ... "

"The real posh one. Huge. Overlooks the castle."

"Oh, the North British Hotel on Princes Street?"

"I don't care for street names," said Abigail. "The one with the clock tower."

"Aye. The North British, ma'am."

"Well, go check in. Have a few days. And that room you're in behind the kitchen? I wouldn't keep my pooch in that. Say, when you get back, I approach your maniac landlord to go fund you proper lodgings for yourself. Somewhere nearby. I've been watching you, Eelee. You're a good egg. You deserve to be happy."

Eilidh gawped, her mouth opening and closing pathetically. She turned to Sarah with the look of someone hoping for answers or the quick end to a terribly distasteful joke.

"I-I am saving for a place, ma'am," mumbled Eilidh. "Putting aside some money. The l-loss of my son, back in . . . the War. I needed time off for nerves, and it set me back."

Abigail looked at Eilidh, her firm strong eyes unblinking and her finger and thumb turning about themselves. Her voice dropped in a way Grimalkin had not heard before. "Well, ma'am, I am most sorry to hear that. That is terrible. I can't begin to imagine. How much you gotta get, savings-wise?"

"About £600 short, miss. For a little place . . . near Blackford Hill."

"If you were to have £5,000 would you have enough to get the house and some nice things for it? A settee and a bed and such?" There was a pause as Abigail flung her head in Sarah's direction. "How much is a house in Edinboro . . . ?"

Eilidh froze, statue-like.

"Um, that is more than enough for a *nice* house with a garden and . . . "

"Great, job done. And think nothing of it. Just keep bringing the cocktails, that's more than enough, thanks. Life has dealt you a tough hand, Eelee. Time to put it right. And this mad age depends on people like you."

Grimalkin, who had been sitting at the foot of the coffee table between the chaise longue and sofa, began to feel prickly with shock, as if he were witnessing a momentous occasion in history. The sort of moment that one had to witness to be believed.

"Oh, miss!"

"Come join us. We're hoping Sarah's husband can make his discovery save lives. Oh, before you do, go get the caviar and crumpets too. All this work has made me hungry."

The Rockefeller Foundation would go on to fund Alexander Fleming's original discovery of penicillin, with the help of Howard Walter Florey and Ernst Boris Chain, a German Jew fleeing Nazi persecution. As of 2020, penicillin is believed to be the biggest biological breakthrough in history, preserving human life and saving an estimated 200 million lives.

Grimalkin's Observations

Decoration: Angles. So many angles!
Humans: Abigail Rockefeller, a rich American, and Sarah Fleming, wife to a scientist.
Technology: The "candlestick radiogram".
Monarch: King George V.

Third Haunting, August 1942

"**D**ON'T DAWDLE, GIRL, TOWELS, *TOWELS!*"
There comes a point in any cat's life where they are wrenched from sleep by a noise so blood-curdling their whole existence flashes before them. Tails are fluffed up, ears are flattened and backs are arched in less time than it takes light to travel a foot. So much for the morning yawn and cleaning regimen on such occasions; these luxuries are well and truly cast aside in place of corrugated hissing mouths and little side scuttles of terror.

So it was for Grimalkin, on a particularly warm day in August 1942.

When his eyes eventually focused, he struggled to understand quite what he was looking at. He was in the front, east-facing bedroom at Marchmont Crescent, he knew that much, as the morning sun was making two oblong yellow prints on the far wall, having travelled through the double set of windows behind him. It was a hot sun, for the cushion on which he awoke felt warm under his fur and was releasing a strong odour of dust in that way that fabric does when it heats up. But this was not the most amiable scent in the room: in fact, there was a dizzying mix of smells, all competing for his nostrils. The familiar odour of furniture polish, linen and what smelt like ethanol. But above all this hung an eye-widening aroma that taunted Grimalkin's nose far more than it would any human's – mammalian blood and sweat. It reminded him of the rare, windless Victorian summer days when Eilidh struggled to air the flat after a boar carcass had been delivered up to the pantry to hang. It positively over-powered the pleasant musk of the furniture polish and hot cushion fabric a hundredfold.

Something was afoot.

With the now-familiar wooziness of recent time travel, Grimalkin rose and attempted to arch his back. It was only then he noticed what was occurring behind him. A woman lay on a bed in an alarming heap of blood-red blankets. A male human, hugely tall with black hair, stooped over the woman and appeared to be frantically inspecting her privates.

Holy mackerel! What is happening? Is she injured? Why are they ... MY WORD, SHE'S SOON TO BE WITH CHILD!

Grimalkin scuttled towards the door then froze. Then scuttled and froze again. He couldn't decide whether to flee or experience this bestial event of human issuing forth another human. Grimalkin himself had fathered several kittens in his time, though took precious little responsibility or interest in any of them. Occasionally, he'd stare at a young taut-limbed feline climbing a tree in the Marchmont Crescent communal garden and the thought would cross his mind *That is one of mine, I wager* ... But he would never think to introduce himself or extend any kind of paternal warmth to the young steer. That is simply not the cat's way. Seeing a human give birth, however, was quite different. He found himself seized with an unquenchable urge to watch the process in full, despite its assault on the senses.

To the left of the bed, there knelt a little woman in a white headdress and smock. She must have been older than the rest of the party as Grimalkin spied wrinkles forming around her mouth and eyes. There was a soothing quality to her – the type of human that any cat immediately wishes to inhabit the lap of for a quick nap. Her eyes glinted a deep auburn when she turned them through sunlight, making the irises look like fresh autumn chestnuts. Now and then, she'd turn to her side and busy herself in a trolley which contained an array of intricately curved items. Something about those metal implements and the woman's face calmed Grimalkin. She was like the captain at the helm of a frigate in a great storm, and the more the woman in labour screamed, the calmer and more composed she seemed.

Beyond the room, Grimalkin could just spy the front door and the stained-glass stag, which appeared to have been cracked and held in place by tape. In the half-light of the hallway, a balding man, in military uniform bearing a flag emblem for a country Grimalkin didn't recognise, was pacing up and down, stiff-legged, and smoking a cigar. Occasionally he'd stop and rock on the balls of his feet while perusing a newspaper which he picked off a hall table. Somehow, Grimalkin just knew instinctively that this was the incoming child's father, and yet he appeared so disinterested in the imminent arrival of his offspring that Grimalkin started to wonder whether he, too, was a cat.

The woman on the bed let out a long, unbroken scream. Grimalkin's ears twisted back, as he retreated under a wardrobe.

"Mrs Raeburn, crack a chloroform ampoule, our lady requires relief," said the tall doctor nasally as he hunched over the foot of the bed like a stalk of corn bowing the wind. "No, no. Abort, too late, too late. Baby's coming! Midwife, by my side, please. Free the cord."

The woman let out one final almighty scream as the baby emerged red and muscular, before being held aloft in the midwife's arms.

There was no cry.

Grimalkin emerged from under the wardrobe and jumped up on the mantelpiece to get a better glimpse of the newborn. It was smeared purple and hanging with viscera.

"W-where's the baby?" said the woman, breathlessly. "Where's my baby, is it alright?"

The midwife and doctor didn't respond. They were busy frantically rubbing the baby's tummy and little feet, which dangled over the side of the instrument trolley by the bedside. Grimalkin spotted the midwife's ruddy face that had lost some of its composure. She was mouthing words silently, which he could just about make out. *Come on, come on, come on.*

"Waaaaaaaaaaaaaaah!" The baby's cry echoed around the room's walls like a banshee.

Cats undergo all this with far more dignity, I must say. Why can't they birth their offspring genially, without fuss, in laundry baskets like us? A smile came to the midwife's face and relief filled the room. The doctor lowered his hands into a metal bowl, sending little ribbons of blood peeling away into the water, before drying his hands in a perfunctory manner on a towel. He peered over to the trolley where the midwife was counting the baby's toes, before looking at a clock on the mantlepiece.

"A healthy baby girl. Time of birth 1.27 p.m., 23 August 1942. Congratulations."

"Thank you," panted the woman. Dark hair flopped stickily around her face, her high-set cheeks reddened, her eyes rolling exhaustedly.

"It'll be the railway journey that brought you on," said the doctor, gathering the implements that lay at the foot of the bed. "From Cornwall, no less? Highly ill-advised and foolhardy, I must say." He placed a small cup against the baby's chest, who was beginning to settle into a mixture of contented gurgles and snorts. "But . . . baby is performing normally. Now, continue with the antibiotic capsules, as your blood infection has not fully rectified, and with the state the nation is in, we cannot have you being hospitalised again. Avoid communal air-raid shelters; they're positively swimming with infection. Oh, and do not move unassisted for the next twenty-four hours. I take it that is all clear, Mrs Ossenbrügge? I *assume* you are married?"

The woman shot the doctor a rueful look.

The doctor dropped his tools into a bag with a disapprovingly loud clatter, before strolling out into the hall, passing the smoking uniformed gentleman with a nod and mumble of "congratulations". The soldier turned his face towards the room in a display of mild interest, before stubbing out his cigarette and ambling into the bedroom like a slothful lion.

"Your daughter, Viktor," said the new mother with a smile. Grimalkin was surprised to hear her speaking in an English accent. A change came over the man. Tears pooled in his eyes, like little beads, as he knelt beside mother and child, kissing them frantically. "You are both zee best of me! Both zee best ov me. Vait till you meet your Czech Babushka and Uncle Sasha, see zehr hills of Pilzen, oh, my glorious, gloooorious girlzees! Glorious girlzees! Vait till Babushka meets you, my precious girlzees!"

New life is always a gift, thought Grimalkin as he considered the long line of outrageous fortune that must have brought this couple to this moment, in this extraordinary building. *How strange that they don't know what has happened in these rooms before them!* He thought of what he had seen so far; its secrets … The conversations of Mr Barrie and the publisher (were they still alive?); Mrs Rockefeller's ring falling beneath the floorboards (was it still there?) and poor Eilidh's bedchamber (was she happier?). Of all these things, though, nothing seemed more magical and remarkable than the birth of a new human in a bed chamber . . . This *very* bed chamber, on this hot afternoon in 1942.

The baby screamed, long and rasping. It was becoming a little too much for Grimalkin to bear. With that, he absented himself to explore the flat, trotting out into the hallway, which was now painted blue and illuminated richly with several handsome lights. He turned into the back bedroom, where he had beheld the Rockefeller lady only five minutes ago. The room had lost much of its former opulence. Instead of the sharp stepped lines, Grimalkin found himself weaving in and out of flat plain pieces of furniture, a wall patterned with tiny repeating flower motifs, and a thick, pale carpet.

What is this witchcraft?

Upon a side table stood a radiogram. At least, it *looked* like a radiogram to Grimalkin. It was made of walnut veneer and had golden mesh stretched over the speakers, three big black dials, and a metal aerial. But there was one key difference – on a tiny little white cube next to the dials it was showing *pictures!* Moving pictures of humans walking . . . A woman singing . . . And now of a dog chasing a ball through long grass.

How have they become so miniature? Have their souls been captured?

A crackly peal of music could be heard trickling out of the speakers at a low volume, alongside a commentary of a human. Grimalkin's head darted left and right like a weathervane in a gale.

The dog is chasing the ball through a meadow . . . and also within this box? But how can dog and man be twain? Their souls split asunder? Oh, what a sordid pantomime of horror this century is turning into, Grimalkin considered, forcing his eyes around the bedroom to stave off the unsettling feeling that the image-box was giving him in the pit of his belly.

Draped over the mattress, the bedspread looked puffy, rather like a cloud, compared to the tight counterpanes of yesteryear. His mind wandered to the Rockefeller ring, and he decided to investigate if it was still under the floorboards after being dropped seven years prior. However, upon heading over to the fireplace, he discovered a chest of drawers had been placed squarely over the site of the hole.

A rustle came from beyond the window as a gust buffeted the great sycamore tree. *Are we past fledgling season, I wonder?*

He jumped up on a chair positioned under the window, which was cushioned with a strange gummy material, a poor imitation of the leather saddles that Eilidh would occasionally wax down in the pantry in Victorian times.

This age has lost its touch on quality, bemoaned Grimalkin. From down the hallway came the muffled cries of the baby interspersed with excitable chatter.

Suddenly, something squirmed under his paws. Grimalkin leaped.

Fie fie! Get thee outside, thy imposter feline! This will forever be MY PATCH.

A tiny black cat was half concealed under a cushion towards the back of the chair. It had clearly been engaged in a mid-afternoon doze before the baby screams had caught its attention, echoing from down the corridor. Naturally, the cat had not felt Grimalkin's presence, although now it rose and turned in a little sleepy semicircle before settling down again to continue the snooze.

Jealousy began to curdle in Grimalkin's breast. A cat's chance observation of another cat is always bound to produce an unedifying series of reactions, but a cat spied *on that cat's turf* prompts a particularly colourful display of machismo. Grimalkin stalked round the little cat, swiping furiously only to have his paw vanish through the dainty beast's face as if it were thin air.

Fie, fie, clear out, you brute! Or if we must spar, let us fight fairly here and now!

Instinctively, Grimalkin raised his tail high into the air and, setting it trembling in the atmosphere like a feather duster, sprayed on the cat's bed. Once again, however, his supernatural form offered no impact on the materiality of his surroundings. So much for marking territory. The curious truth was that Grimalkin felt unable to control his visceral responses to other cats. They were involuntary, just like the poising of his claws when he saw a delicious piece of yarn dangling off the side of a chair. Where he did possess some power as a thinking cat, however, was in how he reflected on his actions. He sat down in front of the little cat, lowered his head, and attempted to purr.

My apologies, young feline. I hereby retract that hasty display of hostility forthwith. Mea culpa. I caused myself a mischief.

The little black cat had no sooner dropped back into a blissful sleep than it raised its head again; a clink of dishes was emanating from the kitchen. It jumped down and trotted expectantly out into the hall, Grimalkin following behind. At this very moment, the tall doctor emerged from the front bedroom, his narrow pencil-like form seeming all the more imposing as it curved gargoyle-like over the trolley of instruments which he trundled towards the front door.

"Err, Sister Raeburn! There is a cat. Sister Raeburn? Can we extricate the cat, please?" He rolled his eyes before opening the door, guiding the little cat out with the side of his shoe. "Animals and infants! When will they realise that the two simply *must not cross!*"

The doctor placed his medical bag out in the communal stairwell, leaving the door ajar as he headed back to the front bedroom to fetch the rest of the equipment. Grimalkin peered through the gap between door and frame. A little summer-scented draught scudded over his nose. And it struck him: he was on his fourth life! Surely this meant he had entered the next phase of Cat-sìth's prophecy? *For three he . . . STRAYS!* Might his path out the door be allowed this time?

He inched closer, feeling trepidation grow as the echo of the stairway amplified the noise of the crashing metal trolley that was coming up behind him from the bedroom.

Oh, drat it. In for a penny, in for a pound, he thought, lowering his head and marching determinedly forward.

He crossed the threshold, unimpeded.

He was free. The year was 1942, and he was outside.

*   *   *

Grimalkin peered through the banisters and down the elegantly curving stairwell. Near the bottom, he spied the little cat running down the final few steps towards the communal front door.

Bring me the world! thought Grimalkin.

With that, he gave chase.

The communal stairwell at Marchmont Crescent was its crowning glory. Huge swathes of cantilevered stairs looped round and round like great twists of ribbon beneath the vibrant green and white wall tiles. New electric lights had been installed on the walls which glowed against the gloom of the cupola glass ceiling above. Trotting down the stairs, Grimalkin noticed that the communal door to the street had been propped open.

He upped his pace, determined not to let the little black cat out of his sight.

A warm breeze whipped his fur as he stepped outside. The feel of cold stone under his paw pads brought him right back to the 1890s, making him feel vertiginous and strange. As a house cat, he had only ever ventured outside in the communal garden of the Marchmont Crescent tenement; as a result, the open street felt dangerous ... Dangerous but exciting. To the right and left the street stood quite still except for the flicker of traffic that could be spied through the railings of the gardens opposite. For a cat, there was nothing else quite like the raw elements tousling against the fur, and Grimalkin felt an immediate wave of gratitude towards Cat-sìth for allowing his ghostly passage to make it out into the wild once more.

This is more like it! he thought, trotting daintily across the cobbles. *This is what I signed up for; not heartache and pain – the great outdoors in a brave new world!*

Venturing over to the kerb, he felt the rising urge to roll himself in the mass of petals and soot that had accumulated in the gutter. He gave in, diving into the sunbaked leaf litter and writhing left and right like a snake until he was fully covered with dust and leaves.

That's most pleasant.

Nearly forgetting what he was meant to be doing, he resumed his pursuit of the little black cat who had just ventured down onto the cobbles in the direction of the main road.

Bruuuuuuuuuummmmm . . .

Grimalkin splayed out his paws. A motorcar had scudded up to him as he'd walked out into the road. Rather than strike him, it mowed right through his ghostly form, leaving a chill frost on his fur. To be invulnerable even to the large human machines should have made Grimalkin feel super-feline; in reality, it just left him feeling numb – a reminder that he had no real impact on the world and people around him. A mute, pathetic observer.

Rallying himself, he scooted up onto the opposite kerb before looking about the great sweeping curve of Marchmont Crescent. Motorcars. *Everywhere.* Ones with fabric roofs; some with great running boards and huge round brass headlamps; others with large grills at their front, like a row of grimacing teeth, and yet more still lining the streets in the distance with large spare tyres mounted awkwardly above their wheel arches.

They look like great overgrown woodlice, thought Grimalkin. *And so many . . . How they pollute the beautiful line of this street! And what have they done with all the horses? Have they killed the horses? Are they all out to pasture? There must be a prolifer-ation of horses somewhere gathering dust behind their ears!*

The smells and sensations were different too. The homely Victorian odours of coal and horse dung that had hung perpetually on the breeze throughout 1890s Edinburgh were now replaced with an odd tangy, polishy scent not too dissim-ilar to Eilidh's tin of household paraffin. The smell was particularly apparent when a motorcar scurried past, which it did in a cloud of green-grey smoke that caught the back of the throat, making Grimalkin sneeze with a great *pffffffftt*.[1]

And say, the iron railings . . . All the iron railings by the front gardens have disappeared, what a beastly decision . . .[2]

Ahead, the little black cat had stopped for a moment beside a particularly handsome chrome-trimmed motorcar to wash its paws. Further on, a great advertising pillar had been positioned on the corner of Marchmont Crescent, fat and filigreed like a great ornate cotton reel. In this age, the posters were in colour. A huge red image had been pasted up in the centre of the pillar, depicting two men with beaming smiles, in peculiar cone-like black hats. Underneath, fancy writing read: *Laurel & Hardy: Hollywood's Funniest Double Act Comes to Edinburgh!* Beside this was a picture of a rainbow crowning a most peculiar array of beings – a lion, a girl and a man who appeared to be dressed in a tin coal scuttle . . . Beneath this one, the title read: *The Wizard of Oz. Weekly Screenings at the Cameo Cinema from only 1/6d.*

---

[1] Grimalkin was of course smelling the leaded fumes of petrol-driven motorcars. Commonplace in 1940s Edinburgh was the Morris Minor and the Hillman Minx.

[2] It was commonplace to remove railings and melt down the iron to use for the manufacture of weaponry during the Second World War. The remnants, or "railing stumps", can still be spied on many Victorian streets around the UK.

What an odd spectacle, thought Grimalkin, his whiskers twitching in thought. *Who on earth would pay 1 and 6 to watch a metal man dance under a rainbow? And what's a cinema, pray . . . Some kind of sordid zoological park?*

But there was something else. A frightful image. It shot fear into Grimalkin's heart, even though he couldn't quite understand it. Pasted above the colourful theatrical faces was a huge poster, aligned slightly at an angle and repeated at several intervals around the billboard. It was of a huge human face with terrifying eyes. All cats are alarmed by prolonged eye contact, but this face had a bewitching effect which both unsettled the heart *and* made it impossible to look away. The figure's mouth was wrapped in a British flag, its eyes blue and piercing. Behind the face was a graphic depiction of a battlefield, strewn with bones and tombstones. The image simply read: "SOMEONE TALKED! Loose Talk Costs Lives."

Grimalkin swallowed. The small cat was still sitting on the corner of the road, sniffing the air serenely, an antidote to the drama and rage of the billboard's images. *Something is not right,* thought Grimalkin. *Some evil is afoot. Either the Empire has fallen, or the Boers have finally washed up on the shores of England.*[3]

---

[3] Grimalkin was probably thinking of the First Boer War of 1880–1881, though knowledge of wars and their respective dates was not his forte.

The little cat resumed its walk. Grimalkin followed, crossing down the path which led to the Meadows via a little alleyway. All along the alley's walls, scrawled writing blazoned out the phrase *"In an Air-Raid, Open Your Door to Passers-by. They Need Shelter Too."* Grimalkin trotted quickly after the little cat, who was upping its pace, stopping only to sniff a little unusual item on the cobbles that could have potential nutritional value. Eventually, the pair turned the corner onto the Meadows, a wonderful wide expanse of green pasture crisscrossed with footpaths.

Ah, the famous Meadows . . . I finally meet you.

The Meadows were an almost mythical space to him, heard only muttered on the tongues of humans who were planning a summertime rendezvous or a game of tennis. Looking at it now, Grimalkin felt immediately more relaxed. Sheep lounged on the warm grass, or nibbled at tufts, and the footpaths of Middle Meadow Walk and Jawbone Walk sliced elegantly through the green. In the middle distance, crowned by Edinburgh Castle, which rose dramatically on its ancient volcanic plug, a group of men played cricket, their white jerseys reflecting the sunlight. It could have been a typical Victorian summer's day, when the stench of belching chimneys and the odour of the Haymarket tanning factory was kept favourably at bay by an easterly breeze licking over the Salisbury Crags.

How nice to be out of that flat and its tawdry furnishings, mused Grimalkin, his little nose twitching up into the breeze as it swept agreeably up his fur. *Such peace and calm! All I must do now is find my Eilidh, and I could reside quite happily in 1942 . . .*

* * *

A short distance on, the little black cat had stopped beside a bench that sat opposite a blue box-like shed that appeared to be the home of a policeman.[4] Clearly, the cat knew the spot well and had been attracted to it for a reason: a bowl of water and plate of what appeared to be fish ends had been placed next to the policeman's box. A delicious fishy scent swept over on the breeze and right up Grimalkin's nose, making him salivate. On the bench opposite, there sat a well-dressed older gentleman, his hat and a battered copy of Emily Brontë's *Wuthering Heights* lying beside him. He stared at the cat with his watery blue eyes, giving a little giggle to himself as it gnawed at the fish ends voraciously.

"Aww, wee Towser, have they nay fed you this morn, doll?" The man had a furry, melancholy kind of voice . . . the kind that was immediately reassuring to a cat's ear. He made a kissing sound with his lips and the cat trotted over for a stroke, its little pink tongue flicking round its mouth for remnant morsels.

---

[4] The police box system was introduced by Edinburgh City Police in 1933. Officers on the beat were able to use them to check in with the police station, via telegraph, for instructions. They were occasionally used also to detain unruly, ale-swilling louts emerging up from the Grassmarket.

The man struck Grimalkin as a decent sort, not wealthy as his collar and sleeves were frayed, but the sort of human who made up for his lack of worldly riches with a lifelong devotion to study and kindness towards others. His face was long, pitted here and there with smallpox scars, and he sported a beard so bushy that it gave the impression that the man possessed no neck at all, much like a teddy bear. His eyes moved slowly, drinking in everything they beheld as if each sight was a rare pleasure. He had that calm, restful manner of a human whose dotage had come upon them with a sort of relief.

Grimalkin walked around to the front of the bench. It was only then he noticed something was wrong. The man was missing part of his left arm, as his sleeve had been pinned back on itself about the elbow. For some reason, this gave him a deeper affection for the man and, as a cat of great insight, Grimalkin had learned to trust his instincts.

I like this gentleman, considered Grimalkin, as he jumped up and trotted onto the man's lap, which was warm and smelled of grass cuttings. The man continued to murmur kindly words to Towser, who nuzzled and purred into the man's breast, her scraggly tail swishing past Grimalkin's eyeline.

Of course, the man had no idea of Grimalkin's presence. But Grimalkin was so starved of human contact and affection that he was positively whisked into a deep, calm sense of relaxation in that blissful moment. He could even trick himself into thinking that *he* was the object of the elderly man's affections, not little Towser. He thought of Cat-sìth

92

and how he would have preferred to renegotiate the terms of his hauntings, not to look and learn from the future but to simply sleep on lovely warm laps on rare, hot Edinburgh summer days throughout the ages. That would be far more pleasant ...

Suddenly Grimalkin's ears flipped back. He leaped up and sprinted away across the Meadows, running for a moment in mid-air. All around, the grass dazzled a bright green. The sheep that had been grazing nearby had darted off as if they had been all pricked with needles at the same time. They now careened towards the avenue of trees which cut the Meadows in two. What Grimalkin had just heard was, quite literally, the worst noise he had ever heard in his life. A noise so awful he could almost feel the blood burning in his eardrums as they vibrated in tune with this awful, synthetic din. The old man had jumped too, sending his hat rolling out over the grass. His fur slowly beginning to resettle on his skin, Grimalkin now looked back up to the line of benches to see the source of the sound: mounted on the roof of the police box was a trumpet ... Not a brass trumpet like one might expect, but an evil electrical trumpet making an up-and-down wailing sound.

Towser, the little cat, was nowhere to be seen. To Grimalkin's astonishment, however, the man remained sitting on the bench. In fact, he was looking up at the blue sky quite calmly, as if his ears were being assaulted by nothing other than the sweet notes of birdsong. As Grimalkin approached, he could even see him smiling weakly to himself, in quiet thought, as if the awful siren had brought about some kind of reverie in him. With a humph, he began scrabbling in his lapel pocket, eventually extracting two purple handkerchiefs which he proceeded to stuff into his ears to block out the din. There he sat almost comically, the purple handkerchiefs flapping merrily in the breeze either side of his head like the ears of a bloodhound.

Soon the whole of the Meadows began to echo with competing sirens all going off in unison.

Honestly, what in the name of all three witches is happening?! thought Grimalkin, as he witnessed several people beginning to move off towards a peculiar hole on the bandstand-side of the Meadows, flanked with stones.[5] An officious-looking man wearing a brown uniform and a helmet marked with a letter 'W' walked in big strides up the path blowing a whistle and sweeping his hands forward. Now humans, young and old, started to emerge from tenement doorways like moles torched out of their homes and began walking in unison towards this strange dug-out space. Some were clutching wicker hampers, a few with random items like picture frames and vases ... Others had cats or dogs in their arms or little wicker baskets.

---

[5] The bandstand in the Meadows was later dismantled in 1950. It was still believed to be held in storage as of 2012.

"Okkkay. Shelters! Step lightly, ladies and gents. Lights out and toooooo the sheeeeeeelters," shouted the man with the whistle.

The warden picked the old man's hat off the grass, giving it back with an offer of his arm for assistance off the bench. But the old man refused, placing his hat back on his head, with a little doff, before raising himself off the bench with a smile, and walking back up the hill towards the tenements in the opposite direction to everyone else, the purple handkerchiefs still flapping about his ears. Eventually, Grimalkin found himself intermingled in the slipstream of stomping feet and commotion. Snatches of half-nervous comments floated through the air: *Ah, kent they'd hit oan Edinburgh soon enough.* And *Did you put out the Cruisie light, Morag?* And a nervous child's voice: *How long will we be down there for, Mummy?*

As was typical for Grimalkin, curiosity trumped fear. He bolted ahead of the crowd and down a set of makeshift steps into the dark underground cavern. A dim bulb glowed from a cable and a radiogram warbled in the corner. Above, a metal ceiling curved into an arch, ridged and fretted like the inside of a cat's mouth. From down here, the electric trumpets sounded mercifully quiet. A large pot of some kind of food was bubbling on a stove and the whole ambience of the space was almost agreeably cat-friendly.

My gosh, beds too? It is a sleeping chamber as well as a common room?

Wooden bunks ran the length of the space, each sporting a little tin box with a red and white cross at the footboard, which swung gently on its nail as people stomped overhead. Along the edges of the upper bunk levels, the shelter's sloped roof curved in so tightly to the bed space that Grimalkin wondered whether he could sleep there comfortably, let alone a human.

"Pack in, pack in, ladies and gentlemen," said the warden man, whose giraffe-like height seemed suddenly ridiculous beneath the gloomy, low ceiling of the shelter. "Get cosy, get cosy. It'll cool down as night falls."

Grimalkin squatted under a bunk as people piled in. Cats, like humans, are tribal creatures forever determining who owns what land, and who should, quite frankly, clear off and find somewhere else to put down their roots. Yet right now, on this warm summer evening in 1942, with some kind of invasion going on – either by the French, the Boers or the Americans, God knew who – Grimalkin was struck by the mighty cross-section of people, all so different, taking up residence in this space all quite affably. There were women in brown overalls with mucky hands who had clearly been tending the vegetable gardens moments before; there were young couples, the ladies in sharply cut mauve jackets with showy hats, the men louche with waxed moustaches, who should have been making their way to the King's Theatre. Then there were workmen in high-waisted trousers and blue shirts with company names stitched on them like Nelson's

Print Works or Bertrams Limited.[6] There were children, some with bare feet and shorts, and others in fine white linen coats who were playing amongst each other, oblivious to class, in a little corner where a selection of wooden toys and books had been stashed.

They're all having a positively capital time, bless Jehovah! thought Grimalkin, feeling a little stirred by the sight. *And no animosity. No spurning betwixt the classes. How queer. What is lighting their spirit, I wonder?*

The chitter of voices fell silent as the warden made an appearance round the corner, ducking through the entrance and stooping under the shallow roof. Grimalkin felt all eyes fall to him, in quiet expectancy, as he removed his helmet and scratched his head, which was glossy with sweat and partially smudged with dirt and grime.

"O-okay, quiet, ladies and gentlemen," he stuttered in a high little voice. "A moment of your time."

The volume in the shelter fell slightly, though whispers and snickers persisted amongst the children like firecrackers stubbornly refusing to be snuffed out.

"Uh ... Uhhm, *quiet, please* ... That *in-in-cludes* children!" repeated the man.

---

[6] By the early twentieth century, Thomas Nelson & Sons rose to become the most successful publishing company in the world. The air-raid shelter attendees Grimalkin saw were possibly on lunch breaks from Nelson's (on Dalkeith Road, east of the Meadows) and Bertrams (on Sciennes Road, to the South).

"Now, ladies and gents, w-welcome to Meadows Shelter 4D. As per usual your full cooperation is most gratefully received in these trying times. H-Hitler is doing his best to wound our resolve, but I'm s-su-sure you'll agree with me, ladies and gents, that the one-balled maniac and his possie have a long way to go before breaking *our* spirits!" There was a gentle, yet affirmative murmur of "Yes" together with a few giggles. "Now, if I can just ask that ... "

He broke off, turning to look over his shoulder. From above there came the frantic commotion of footsteps. The occupants of the shelter looked at the gloomy opening with a mixture of curiosity and trepidation. Moments later, around the corner, stumbling and arguing, came a clutch of people. Grimalkin recognised them immediately as the current residents of Marchmont Crescent – the new parents: Viktor, who had a heavy bag over his shoulder with the initials "RAF" stitched on it, his wife, the baby and Sister Raeburn. But someone else was accompanying them; an old woman, bent over with a scarf wrapped tightly around her head. In Grimalkin's eyes, she seemed a little witch-like, as if she had just leaped out of the pages of a human child's fairy tale. She walked shakily but confidently into the heart of the shelter as if wholly used to the business of entering a hole in a field with a group of strangers. On seeing her, and hearing the gurgle of the baby, several of the shelter occupants shuffled to make space.

"Mrs Ossenbrügge, allow me to hold the baby," said Mrs Raeburn. The father wafted her hand away, speaking rather too loudly for the situation and setting: "Nooo, no, stupid nurse! Don't zey tell you this in Scotland. Ze bébé must be with za mozzer. Leave 'er! Leave 'er alone!"

They jostled along the shelter. In a far corner, a little girl in school uniform cooed at the baby, who gurgled away in a tightly swaddled blanket, its mother's exhausted face still pale with greasy fronds of matted hair sticking alongside her cheeks and temples.

The warden man shuffled awkwardly, eyeing the late arrivals with annoyance for throwing off his little speech.

"Right, um. G-good you made it, good you made it, yes. Um, now, as I was saying, ladies and gents, welcome to Meadows Shelter 4D . . . "

"My congratulations, madam," said a posh-looking lady, in a low voice, turning to the mother. "How old?"

"Just minutes, just minutes old!" butted in Viktor. "Born at 1.27 in ze afternoon. My bébé! And she is ze best of me!" The man lit up a cigar, immediately disappearing in a thick cloud of smoke.

"Yes, *th-thank you*," said the warden pointedly, his hunched giraffe-like neck under the roof seeming all the more comic as his patience ran thin. "As I was about to co-communicate, *if I may* . . . " He reached into his pocket and extracted a little collection of booklets, which he fanned out and presented to the assembled party with grave importance. "These here safety pamphlets must be studied intimately, in order that you know how to behave if shelter safety is compromised."

"Poppy coddles," shouted Viktor, interrupting the warden. "Complete poppy coddles!"

"I do b-beg your pardon?" said the warden, aghast.

"Vot is there to know?! Either vee get hit by zee Luftwaffe, in vich case *keeeeeek*—" He moved his hand across his throat in a slashing action "—or vee do not get hit by zee Luftwaffe and vee get to live another day. Shelter safety. It iz poppy coddles!"

"I believe it's a little bit more c-complicated than that, sir," hissed the warden, his lower jaw jutting with pent-up anger as several other shelter occupants began giggling at Viktor's comments.

"Poppy coddles and balder-snatch, of *course it izzz*," said Viktor, growing in stature as he felt the eyes of the assembled party turn on him. "I am only saying vot zees people are thinking, but they are from Edinburo so they are too shy. Look I have a bébé, you think I vould'nt care about her safety? Anyvay, they are not vanting us here anyvay. They are vanting to hit zee docks in Glasgow."

"W-with respect, sir ... " stuttered the warden.

"Anyway, important matters!" shouted Viktor "Who vants Pilzner? And Guláš! My Babushka's Guláš is za best in Czechoslovakia, the mayor of Brno says so!"

The little old lady, Viktor's "Babushka", seemed to spring to life upon hearing the word "Guláš", and began rummaging in the RAF bag, pulling out a variety of little plates and bottles, and offering them around.

A buzz of excitement swept through the shelter like a warm breeze. The little girl in school uniform trotted over to look in the old Babushka's bag. Smiling, Viktor's Babushka patted the side of her cheek with hands so antique and wrinkled that her knuckles had gone pearly-white, and her veins were visible and blue beneath the skin. She muttered something to the little girl Grimalkin couldn't understand. "Nádherné dítě! Nádherné dítě!" Then from the bag, she produced a little rag doll, small but perfectly detailed in a red dress with gold stitching on the hem. The little girl grinned, bouncing on the spot.

A calm fell across the shelter. People began to talk among themselves and eat. Some exchanged stories of the day; others laughed at the ridiculousness of the situation. *Food brings the humans together,* thought Grimalkin, musing for a moment how different it was among cats. Indeed, the smells coming from the Babushka's cooking seemed exotic and heady to Grimalkin, as if they were infused with the same mix of ingredients that made Babushka herself so sturdy, and Viktor so headstrong. It was the food of another land and its people.

Viktor turned to his wife and baby, kissing them both with great gentleness. The baby looked around, its little podgy alabaster cheeks glowing in the dim light. A lively little woman, with a chubby face and blue-grey eyes, leaned over the baby and sang a nursery rhyme: "Ally bally, ally bally bee, Sittin' on yer mammy's knee, Greetin' for a wee bawbee, Tae buy some Coulter's candy."

Viktor rose and headed to the warden, who was sitting alone at the foot of the shelter stairwell and offered him a beer and plate of food which he accepted with a half-smile and nod.

"Mr Ossenbrügge, Mr Ossenbrügge. A moment of your time." Sister Raeburn was waving at Viktor, her hand in one of the Red Cross boxes at the footboard of a bunk bed.

"Mr Ossenbrügge, those medicines, please?"

Viktor broke off with a raise of his finger, stepping over to the bag and extracting a brown vial of tablets from a side pocket. He opened the vial and gave two to the nurse, who poured a cup of water from a steel jug at her foot and took out a little brown bottle labelled "Morphine Tartrate". Viktor offered his wife the tablets.

"Thank you," panted the woman, her brow contorted with pain. "Viktor, darling, hold my hand." She took the morphine tablet from the nurse before swallowing the pills handed to her by Viktor with a swig of water and a backwards jerk of the head.

"I daren't ask where you procured these penicillin tablets from, Mr Ossenbrügge," said Nurse Raeburn, her red face pinched with a wry smile. "But I can assure you, whole-heartedly ... These last two weeks they have saved your wife and baby's lives."

Grimalkin's Observations

Decoration: Uncomfortable rubbery chairs.
Humans: Viktor Ossenbrügge, wife, Sister Raeburn.
Technology: Radiogram with pictures! Warbling siren of hell.
Monarch: King George VI.

Fourth Haunting,
June 1953

"WOOF, WOOF!"

Grimalkin's eyes were green orbs before he could draw breath. The crooked end of his tail flicked like a rattlesnake, and all along his back, his fur had fluffed up. If anything was likely to stir a cat from a supernatural slumber in short order, it'd be the bark of a dog.

Confounded scoundrel! Show your dreadful face. I will take you to the deuce and back, I tell you!

We have all seen a cat attempting to locate the source of a threat and it is a comic charade, to say the least. Grimalkin barely had time to notice he was in Marchmont Crescent's front room before he was ducking in and out of furniture, leaping on tables and mousing behind the settee, all to find the source of the barking. He scarcely noticed the string of Union Jack flags, strung together in little triangles, from one end of the bay window to the next, nor the glittering crystal cake stands set on the table, each proudly displaying a cloud of butter-coloured sponge and laced with cream and treacly lumps of apricot.

Canine, show thy brutish face! Let us duel to the death here and now!

It was no use. There was no dog to be found. Feeling woozy with adrenaline and stress, Grimalkin eventually perched his rear end down nervously next to a small white radiogram. A woman's voice warbled through the meshed speaker in the chippering final bars of a song: "How much is that doggie in the window? I do hope that doggie's for sale."

Grimalkin half-closed his eyes, feeling stupid.

It was a radio dog. Grimalkin, you fool, the dog was on the wretched radiogram. My, am I pleased no beast oversaw that little escapade.

His tail fluff lost its spikiness as his gaze dropped sheepishly towards his front paws.

The radiogram's warble shifted to the voice of a man. Grimalkin swivelled his right ear to listen:

"And that was *'How Much Is That Doggie in the Window?'*[1] and what a jolly, toe-tapping number with which to commence coronation festivities on this day of our Lord.

---

[1] Lita Roza's version of *(How Much Is) That Doggie in the Window?* hit number 1 on 24 April 1953.

I ought to reassure our listeners that while Prince Philip has campaigned tirelessly to broadcast today's auspicious events via your television sets, our loyal radiogram listeners will still be catered for as we deliver you all the latest concerning the anointing of Princess Elizabeth, direct from Westminster Abbey from eleven o'clock – the location of every royal coronation in England since 1066. I dare say we will all remember where we were on this glorious occasion today, 2 June 1953. I pass you off now to Mary Hill for *Woman's Hour . . .* "

Grimalkin lolloped down onto the floor, where a big rug with a deep pile tickled his feet and ankles. *Celebrations, coronations and dogs barking down the radio. What a tawdry age. I assume the poor old king must be dead, alas. I see none of them have outdone our gracious Victoria in years of reign. Queen Elizabeth, indeed . . . she'll under-reign gracious Victoria too, you mark my paws.*

From behind the stand of sickly-looking cakes, a lady entered accompanied by two bounding children. They were carrying a large glass jar of what appeared to be juice that slurped and sloshed over the lip as the children bounced and screeched with excitement.

"Now, Roy, I'm telling you, you're cruising for a bruising. You'll make yourself sick with all this jigging about. Get a J-Cloth and mop up that mess right now. Isla, Isla, put that down *this instant.*"

"But, Mum, you said . . . "

"No cake till the street party, Isla. I told you as much. Now go and get changed. The goodly residents of Marchmont Crescent deserve more than to see you bounding around in the near-altogether. Shoo shoo!"

The two children ran out and Grimalkin peeked around the living room walls. There was a unkept, grubby feel to the decor and it was probably the first occasion Grimalkin recalled the great old living room looking uncared for. The furniture, formerly opulent and plush through the ages, looked cheap and somehow futile, as if it would be better placed in a garden shed or veterinary practice. The walls had been painted pale green, seemingly in haste as there were little blotches here and there, and two standard lamps stood either side of the settee, with shades of frayed silk that was browning in patches like overripe fruit. There was a fishy, musty scent in the air,[2] and the once-grand fireplace with its sweeping surround had been boxed in.

Either they have no means or are exceptionally ill-bred, considered Grimalkin haughtily.

He nosed into the hallway, spying a child's tricycle shoved into the box room – Eilidh's former sleeping quarters – along with several brown boxes piled haphazardly. The hall was dark, only a thin shaft of morning light crept under the doors of the

---

[2] Potentially the odour of French Bakelite, whose smell is often likened to that of rotten milk.

east-facing rooms, illuminating the auburn floorboards, which were scuffed and dented. The stained-glass stag, above the front door, had been nearly completely coated with a skim of dust. Snooping through into the front bedroom, Grimalkin was astonished to find *this* space practically unchanged since he had seen the baby delivered there in the previous decade.

They've scarcely mopped the blood off the floors! he thought with a little jump as he could swear he saw a cockroach scuttling through a crack beside the fireplace. As he trotted round to sniff the spot for any cockroachy odours, he did notice one difference – the counterpane that hung limply over the bed was patterned with a preponderance of palm tree images which clashed, in a ghastly way, with the chimney breast that had been painted orange and adorned with three bird ornaments in differing stages of flight.

Hmmm. It all feels a little threadbare. That ring under the floorboards in the back bedroom would come in useful for this family, I shouldn't wonder . . .

"Roy! Isla! Come help me with the custard slices!"

Grimalkin trotted down to the kitchen in the direction of the voice – a walk he could've done with his eyes closed.

"Here, Isla, take these. Watch the curried sauce, darling, it'll slurp. Oh, wonderful little sombrero, Roy, very fetching! Isla, I won't tell you again, if you ruin that petticoat, that is your last! We're out of credit at the dressmakers until the New Year. No, Roy, we've no time now, we need to hurry. Now be good, both of you, and don't show us up in front of all of Marchmont."

109

Before Grimalkin had the chance to scope out the kitchen, he was swept in the slipstream of the departing family, their food parcels and outfits all balancing and jostling precariously as they shuttled out the door into the communal stairwell like a poorly rehearsed circus act.

Well, if I must stray, I might as well stray with these types, infuriating as they seem, thought Grimalkin. *I do hope they have some clue as to Eilidh's whereabouts to make the venture worth it.*

The lady pulled shut the door behind his tail. Outside there was a strange charge of emotions in the air. A warble of music could be heard sweeping up the streets from the Meadows, and the same Union Jack bunting that was strung across the front window at Marchmont Crescent was twisted between railings and streetlamps. One man, in a flamboyant suit and red, white and blue striped tie was up a telegraph pole, his legs clung round it like a monkey, tugging on an unwilling string of flags from a lamp post opposite. "Brian, loosen that end, would ye?" he called.

The assemblage of people on the street was the biggest Grimalkin had ever seen. In his earlier hauntings the sheer sight of such a mass of humans would have made him skulk away, but he was getting used to his superpowers. He felt buoyed and brave. And somehow he just knew that among this crowd of people lay a clue as to his dear Eilidh's whereabouts, if she was indeed alive.

If only there was a way I could speak! mused Grimalkin, feeling himself longing for the powers of verbal communication for the first time ever.

Turning to his right, he was stunned to see a huge table, or indeed a series of tables, almost as long as the street itself draped in a haphazard assortment of tablecloths. On seeing the kaleidoscope of colour and jubilation, the little children from Marchmont Crescent immediately shrieked and ran ahead, whooping and cooing at their friends who sat at one of the tables.

"Okay, so, ladies and gentlemen, quiet, please!" A little square-faced, bearded man in a coloured suit bounced on the scene, stepping upon a milk crate to give himself some height. With each word, he shook his right hand for emphasis as if scrubbing an invisible work surface in mid-air. "Okay, please, shush shuuush, quiet or we'll all hear hee-bloody-haw!"

Grimalkin couldn't quite decide whether his clown-like garb and lively face was a charming addition to the spirit of the occasion or a downright abomination to the rules of fashion and decency. On top of his head, there perched a little pork-pie hat like a snuffer on a candle. He tried one final time to subdue the crowd. "Okay, jings, you chatterboxes! Shhhh! Okay, thank you. Welcome to the Coronation Celebrations of Marchmont Crescent. I hope and trust we'll all have a fabby time today as we see in our wonderful wee Princess Elizabeth, may she reign forever."

A whoop went up among the crowd.

"And by jings do we need something to lighten the mood of that ruddy baldy-nut Churchill's ration crusade." Laughter burst out mixed with a cheer that sounded to Grimalkin already a little bit drunken. "Now, to business. I kindly remind you that myself Jimmy McTulloch and Sally down at the Thirlestane Road end ... Can you hear me, Sally?"

"Yes!" came back a faint cry.

"Thank goodness for that, I thought she'd nabbed that new television machine and run off ... So, myself and Sally will be checking coupons to make sure you're all residents from here. If you're nay residents, I kindly ask you to jog on to another party as I'm sure you'll appreciate we only have so much to go around. Okay, finally, can I hear it from the Hamiltons of Mansionhouse Road?" A big cheer went up halfway along the table, from an especially made-up group of people wearing what appeared to be miniature golden top hats.

"The Hamiltons have kindly brought their new aforementioned television machine out for an airing. Now I know some of you are worried about the radiation. I am assured they are perfectly safe, and just like the radio, the princess will definitely, *definitely* not be able to hear us. We can only hear her. One-way communication. Hmm-hmmm. So, when the clock strikes 11.15, we're going to tune into the Abbey to listen to the day's events. But until then get some scran in your wee selves. Buon appetito and may God save our new queen!"

Grimalkin flinched as a couple of firecrackers went off, sending an arc of red ribbon in the air. Boys, clearly ne're-do-wells from neighbouring parts of Edinburgh, cycled scampishly up and down in bedraggled trousers and shirts, grabbing the odd cake from the table before being shooed away by the adults. Dogs barked, and high up in the tenement windows, Grimalkin spied several cats eying the scene archly, clearly relieved they were indoors rather than out.

I must say, this smells positively revolting, thought Grimalkin, scrambling up the paper tablecloth to get a better look at the various steaming dishes of food. Out in front of his paws, the long stretch of tables jaggled their way in front of him like a crooked path. He made his way down the table, nosing in and out of various high-sided casserole pots and dishes to examine their contents.

There are some occasions when a cat shows immediate repulsion to food on account of it being unfit for the consumption of *any* self-respecting beast. On these occasions, the assembled mass of so-called nutrition is so abhorrent that the cat in question will immediately reel back and retch, often producing a "furball of disapproval" in the process. What Grimalkin saw along the table on that June Coronation Day of 1953 was nothing more than a smorgasbord of pure alimentary horror. Carrots and parsnips lay slopped over each other, blanched of their colour, and overcooked to the point of seeming somehow out of focus. Cakes and jellies had been dyed in the colours of the Union Jack; but the once-solid red, white and blue colourings had run into each other, turning the jellies into a liver-coloured slop, resembling a sea-anemone caught up in an oil slick. It was a sight that made Grimalkin feel nauseous, despite having built a stomach that could happily withstand two-week-old squirrel offal in the 1890s. And here, next to his paws, sat a little pyramid of sandwiches cut into triangles on a plastic plate. He sniffed the bread only to lurch back with a noseful of an odd, synthetic smell that appeared to be emanating from some canary-yellow replacement for butter between the slices. Cans stood, like sentinels, between the party hats and dishes, with equally dubious names like Crest Top Collard Greens and Crest Top Pork & Beans.

What a vile repast, thought Grimalkin at the heady mix of sweet and fatted odours that knitted through the air. He retched in that lavish cat way, again grateful that none of the assembled party could see him.

Suddenly, as people started to lean in grabbing plates and casserole dishes, something yet more astonishing happened. The humans began to eat with such a frantic pace that Grimalkin started to think they mustn't have eaten for several days prior.

Has fasting become a prerequisite for swearing in a new monarch? Why are they so hungry? I remember venison cutlets on the occasion of Queen Victoria's Diamond Jubilee in 1897.

Adults grabbed and scooped and dolloped and gobbled, while children stretched their mucky hands into the centre of the table to grab a fistful of pie or pudding. Here and there, with a furtive look to their neighbours, several humans even appeared to be *stealing* food, smuggling it in bags and dishes concealed at their feet. It was odd and unseemly to behold, reminding Grimalkin of a gathering of stray dogs fighting over a carcass.

With a little leap onto a chair, Jim made a reappearance, his hand and outstretched finger jiggling frantically. "Uh, uh, uh. I know times are tough with rations, ladies and gentleman, but try to leave enough to go around or we'll be in a right boorach! No more than your share! *Oi!* I'm watching you, Gladstone Terrace contingent!"

Several minutes passed as the voices and chatter fell beneath the clinks and clangs of rapidly moving cutlery. From the end of the street came the *chug-ug-ug-ug* of a motorcar, turning a corner and pulling up. A lady emerged, waving to Jim McTulloch, who bounced up and cantered along the street. A cat's eyes can see further than a human's, but even Grimalkin struggled to see what the lady passed over to Jim. It appeared to be a plate, holding some kind of mound covered with a tea towel.

And then, an aroma of *pure deliciousness* swept through the air. A scent so scrummy and powerful that Grimalkin felt nearly knocked sideways with tummy-churning hunger ... and *nostalgia.*

That's an Eilidh pie! Grimalkin shivered with a mixture of nostalgia and joy, right down to the tip of his tail and the apex of his ears. *I'd bet my tail on it! I could pick that odour out if it were the last on earth – it's Eilidh's steak and haggis recipe ... I can smell the extra lard and mace!*

For the moment, the feasting humans had detected nothing. Only a cat's nose could pick up a waft so acutely immediately following its arrival. Then heads started to turn towards the little tea-towel-covered mound, which already surpassed everything else on the table from the aroma alone.

Grimalkin skulked down the centre of the tables, eyeing the faces of people as he went. On closer inspection, there was a pallidness to many of the visages – a pointed, drawn look to the children, and a haunted jitteriness to some of the men. It belied a life of poor diet and scarcity of food. It lurked behind the eyes of the revellers, temporarily concealed by the smiles of celebration on this special day.

Some of these men must have fought in the war that took Eilidh's son, thought Grimalkin, as he trotted anonymously past. They were a generation of survivors, raising a generation of indestructible children, hell-bent on survival despite the looming spectre of recent events.

Just as he reached the end of the line of tables, Jim McTulloch removed the tea towel from the top of the pie. That the tea towel depicted scenes of Eilidh's native Ayrshire only confirmed the identity of the pie's maker all the more in Grimalkin's mind. This was proof. This was proof that Eilidh *still lived.* She was no longer in the service of Marchmont Crescent, but she was probably in Marchmont, or nearby. Grimalkin spied Eilidh's trademark pastry pattern around the top of the pie – the four flower buds, made with the end of the fork, pushed at intervals around the pie's circumference, like bearings on a compass.

He sniffed the top and tried to bite into it. But, cruelly, his mouth simply gave way. This would normally have been torturous were it not that Grimalkin was far too buoyed on the sure and certain knowledge that Eilidh still must be alive.

Well, if I am free to roam in this life, I am resolved to find Eilidh, even if I must ward off sleep for days. I will not leave this life until we lock eyes!

* * *

Grimalkin gazed at the tenements curving away along Marchmont Crescent. The turreted roofs of the upper flats speared up into a sky that was turning ominously dark. Rain was coming, and if Grimalkin knew one thing, it was that an Edinburgh summer downpour was a kind of meteorological purgatory that had to be experienced to be believed. Hailstones the size of tennis balls would arrive out of nowhere and pelt down so forcefully on his cat head that he'd feel dizzy and sick.

He upped his pace along Marchmont Crescent, on a mission. His fur gratefully insensitive to the first fat drops of rain, he tried to cast his mind back to 1935, when he had chanced upon Eilidh's diary ... *Where was it she said she dreamed of living? Glenesk? Or was it Glenisla? I wonder if that Rockefeller lady made true on her promise of money?* Grimalkin's memories rolled in indistinctly upon themselves like curling scoops of butter under a passing knife.

It was Glen-something, I recall . . . thought Grimalkin as he glided through a flagstone wall and onto the narrow, cobbled Thirlestane Lane. He eyed the stable blocks along the length of the gloomy little road, wondering which one he had been born in back in 1887. Today, the stable doors were losing their paint, or had rotted through. Some stables had had their doors wrenched clean off, their insides made into little homes for motorcars who sheltered cosily among canisters of paraffin and diesel like little mice. On warmer evenings, the dairy further along would leave pails of milk for the street cats to lap at. Now it was shut up and derelict, its ribbed system of rafters and beams exposed like a skeleton to nesting birds and ivy.

Glen, glen . . . glen-something.

A childish yelp wafted up the road. Grimalkin turned his head to see the lady he had awoken to in the flat. She was leaning, one-handed, against a lamp post as her daughter was being sick into the gutter. "Oh, Isla, you silly, silly thing. Too much cake! Roy, take your sister over to Janis's, she'll have some chamomile tea."

Isla! thought Grimalkin suddenly. *Eilidh had wanted to move to Glenisla Gardens!*

Grimalkin upped his pace and turned down the alley beside the cemetery just as the rain began to fall in torrents. Being a cartographer, his late master Mr Calvert always had plenty of maps strewn about the flat, meaning Grimalkin had picked up a surprising amount of knowledge of the local roads, streets and alleys without ever having walked them himself. He knew, for instance, that Glenisla Gardens was a crooked little road located in a hollow beyond Grange cemetery, which would be just beyond this little passageway where he was now. Tall mossy stone walls loomed either side of him as he upped his pace, trotting alongside a red postbox which still bore Queen Victoria's insignia *VR*.

Halfway down, Grimalkin turned to his left, dissolving through the stone wall into an immaculately appointed back garden; each rhododendron and acacia, each cube of lawn and vivid tulip petal was so perfectly appointed, pruned and ordered that Grimalkin felt almost taken aback. He was now in the Grange; the poshest part of town.[3] Legend has it that the cats down here in Victorian times would almost exclusively be pedigree. Indeed, one wealthy old family back in 1894 had, according to local gossip at the time, decorated an entire stable, beside a garage, specifically for their cats. The butler, Mr Afflick, was apparently very kind to local cats, often surreptitiously letting in strays with an affectionate call of, "I dare say, you're set on stealing wee Luna's cream," or "You're a sleekit wee thing, here, have some victual. Don't go spreading it around, mind, and make scarce or I'll be out of a position by lunch time."

---

[3] By chance, Grimalkin happens to have strayed into the garden of a house formerly belonging to Donald Mackinnon Macalister, an early minister of the Free Church of Scotland (1832–1909).

In the distance the peals and screeches of the street parties could be heard threading through the air. But down here all was quiet. The garden was damp and vivid green with the recent rain. Here and there abandoned furniture lay scattered on the streets, suggesting the jubilee celebrants had retreated inside to avoid the shower. Grimalkin peered in through the tall windows of an ominous-looking house with multiple turrets that seemed to scrape savagely against the stormy sky above. Inside he could hear laughter as heads bobbed in and out of view behind a huge oval pane of stained glass.

I wonder how this wartime has affected these well-to-do residents? mused Grimalkin, trotting up the back garden steps between two great stone lion heads. A quick nudge against the brickwork and he glided straight on through.

* * *

By Jove, it's a PALACE in here! thought Grimalkin, gawping around a humungous drawing room that could possibly have fitted half of the Marchmont Crescent flat into it. A great baroque cornice looped and swirled around the top edges of the ceiling to a bay window where a grand piano stood, its lid open ostentatiously. People stood in various little clutches talking amongst themselves. Grimalkin trotted up to eavesdrop on a conversation taking place in an alcove behind the piano. Two ladies stood talking intently; the first, bony and upright with a long, thin face, was clutching a flute of champagne whose apricot hue offered all the colour that her clothes and greyish skin lacked. The other was a smaller, mousy-looking woman with painfully symmetrical hair and a podgy, busy-looking face.

"And the nonsense with the pillar boxes, Margaret, bearing the royal cypher of *EIIR*. I mean, I ask you! Some people will never be satisfied, *never*. The one on St Catherine's Place – defaced with obscenity! As are the ones on Findhorn Place and Whitehouse Loan. All ruined. I mean, she is our queen, she is *Scotland's queen*. The rest of the scoundrels will just have to get used to it or go and live somewhere else."

"Absolutely, Audrey, I completely agree," said the mousy lady with perfect hair.

"We have been a union of nations since 1707. So as far as I'm concerned, Elizabeth (may she live forever) *is* the second Elizabeth of Scotland. And just because Elizabeth I (may God rest her soul) preceded that union of our current Elizabeth II (may she live forever) does not mean she ought not to benefit from the protocol of *this* union. She is Scotland's second Elizabeth."[4]

---

[4] The women are referencing the Pillar Box Wars of the 1950s during which Elizabeth Windsor's status as the second Queen Elizabeth to rule over the UK was challenged in Scotland. Many pillar boxes in Scotland with the new royal cypher were vandalised at this time (though clearly not by women like this).

"Completely correct, Audrey. The British monarchy is as old as the hearth. *Imagine* trying to go it alone. The *idea!*"

"Absolutely, absolutely. Why, they couldn't!"

How ridiculous. This feels like a conversation out of the last century! thought Grimalkin, who was beginning to surprise himself at how un-Victorian he was starting to feel as his hauntings progressed. What once seemed like great edicts of righteous discussion now seemed silly and naïve when viewed in the context of his hauntings of 1909, 1935 and 1942. Even the way they spoke seemed puffed up and bothersome. *Did I really used to be that pompous? Am I becoming, dare I say it, "modern"?* A faint smell of baking bread reminded his tummy of the mission to locate Eilidh and check how she now lived. He departed the house through the front door and trotted down over the cobbles, which now glistened in a surprise sunburst.

Glenisla Gardens is hidden away in a little thicket between the handsome roads and villas of the Grange. Many Edinburgh residents would not even know it existed. As Grimalkin glided past the road sign and down into the glen of nestled cottages, it felt like he was stepping out of Edinburgh and into the deepest countryside. He recalled the shock of seeing Eilidh so aged in 1935; how dirty her hands looked and how sad her eyes had been from what he would go on to discover was the loss of her son in a war. If Grimalkin were to see her now – if she *had* indeed bought a house here with the Rockefeller lady's money – how would her life have changed?

She will not have adopted airs and graces, like those soppy noodles up the road, mused Grimalkin. *She is far too wise and wedded to her class.*

But why had she not come up to the party at Marchmont Crescent? Could she not get an hour off from her position to partake in the celebrations like everyone else in the city?

Why, her tyrant employer would have ME to answer to if that were the case, seethed Grimalkin in a sudden burst of loyal anger.

At the foot of the gardens, hidden round a corner, a small salmon-coloured cottage was set back a little from the rest. A pale blue door sat perfectly in its centre, crowned by a great spray of ivy. It made Grimalkin feel warm just to behold it. In the windows either side, a minuscule set of striped curtains were pulled aside, revealing an earthenware pot of geraniums sat on each windowsill, flickering in and out of view behind bobbing hydrangea blooms. But it was the perfectly polished brass door knocker – a true Eilidh giveaway – that confirmed, beyond any doubt, this was Eilidh's home. It put to shame all the other brasswork on the other houses, such was its dazzling shine.

She is here and she lives!

Grimalkin circled the house. A length of wisteria rained purple buds on a paved side alley leading to the back garden. There at the far end of the lawn were the remains of what was presumably Eilidh's air-raid shelter from the second of the two big wars that had hit this century.

123

But there was something else. Something shocking. A sombre feeling came over Grimalkin. The back garden, unlike the front, was in complete and utter disorder. In every corner and on every patch of grass, fossilised tools and washing items lay strewn haphazardly into middens. Something wasn't right. Something didn't *feel* right. A knot formed in Grimalkin's belly, making his ears and body flatten to the ground. Despite not being able to feel anything beneath his paws, the sensation of stepping over this splinter-infested melee of rusty pots, bags of old nails and split broom handles made him wince. He half expected his supernatural immunity to desert him and to feel a burst of pain exploding on his paw as a shard of glass sliced into his tender pads. He recognised the brushes and coal scuttle; the tins of Dustbane Sweeping Compound, Fiebing's Saddle Soap, and of course the tins of Brasso. Under a pear tree beside the stone perimeter wall, he even noticed some of Eilidh's clothes – the white headdress and her little shoes, once bright black, now decayed and falling to pieces.

Eilidh would never live like this. Something is not up to dick . . .[5]

At that moment, Grimalkin spied that the back door to the property was ajar. Someone must be home. Carefully, he trotted over the mouldering items, and slunk through the

---

[5] Victorian phrase meaning "not very well".

door, finding himself in a little pantry. Grimalkin gazed around in astonishment. A stone sink and draining board squatted in the gloom while a Sheila Maid swayed above on the incoming breeze from the back garden, its drying tea towels dangling down limply like sails. Gas was licking gently under a kettle on the hob, which sizzled with the hush of a near-boil. There was something about the way things were arranged that made Grimalkin think someone else was living here, as well as Eilidh: the tea towels, while definitely her preferred pattern, were folded into rectangles rather than triangles, and the crockery was arranged in size order rather than colour order as was Eilidh's preference.

Grimalkin walked further into the house, nervous at the prospect of what he'd see next. He ventured up the stairs, in that wide-eyed faltering way typical of all cats when they enter a new dwelling space. As he neared the top landing, the smell of medicine and earthiness caught his nostrils, mixed with the more familiar Eilidh smells of beeswax polish. There was a murmur of chatter creeping around a half-opened door. He followed the sound until he reached the front bedroom – the one with the beautiful gable end, overlooking a little spinney of trees opposite. An elderly man was sitting alongside a bed, still and slightly curve-backed like a statue in a museum. The bed itself was unkept – little stains bloomed here and there where tea or supper had spilled on the eiderdown and been dabbed off. The room seemed to glitter ethereally with the post-rain light which poured in through the window. Outside, the jeers and screams of street parties could still be heard alongside the crackle of wireless radios turned up to their maximum volume.

And in the bed, her head cowed and her hands lying slate-grey and limp, was Eilidh.

Eilidh!

There was something vague and unsettling about her face. She seemed to Grimalkin to be haunted around the eyes, and her once rosy cheeks, previously conspicuous against her swan-white skin, now seemed flushed, sticky and pallid. Her breathing was laboured; her eyes unfocused and watery, like a fish's, as they disappeared in and out of sight beneath their lids.

"Reggie, is there someone else here?" she asked weakly.

The old man leaned in, picking up her hand in his. He shuffled the stool he was sitting on towards her gently. "Um, no, no, my darling, it's just us."

"The window? Have you opened another ... those cheers?"

"No, my wee scone, I've not changed a thing. That's just the coronation revellers. Queen Elizabeth's coronation. It's just the two of us, darling. Always and ever. Just the two of us, my little E." The man bit his lip and looked down. "Are you quite comfortable, my little E?"

"Yes, quite comfortable; just fair peely-wally," faltered Eilidh breathily.

"Is there anyone you'd like me to bring to pay a visit, little E, dear? I will do all in my power to bring anyone ye wish to see."

Grimalkin jumped up on the bed and sat before Eilidh, his front legs positioned perfectly together, and his eyes unblinking and still on his old, dear human companion. The human to whom he owed his life and whose every pain and joy had attended him with each haunting. It was always agonising for Grimalkin to witness Eilidh at a ghostly remove, but this was the toughest occasion of all. What if he never saw her again after today? Eilidh's eyes rolled around the room, seeming to lose focus. Her hair, which the man had evidently attempted to keep in style, fell loose from its pin near Eilidh's forehead. The man quickly rose and pinned it back in place. Eilidh smiled.

"You know, Reg, it's awffy, awffy queer ... "

"What is, my dear?"

"That wee cat I rescued with Maw, ken way back in 1887, and I brought to live at Marchmont Crescent. When I was wie my maw on apprentice."

"Oh, aye," said the man, his brows knitting. "Aye, the wee um ... the wee Grimalkin, wis it? Born out on Thirlestane Lane?"

"Aye. Well, I wouldnae be damned if he wisnae among us here and now. In this very room!"

The old man smiled with a minor bow of the head, the top of his shirt disappearing under his wide, bearded chin.

And it was in that moment Grimalkin recognised him. He was the same gentleman he had met on the bench in 1942, who had been feeding the little black cat and refused to enter the air-raid shelter! Now Grimalkin was surprised he didn't

127

recognise the man sooner – the little teddy bear neck disappearing under his beard (which had now turned a pure white), the mournful voice and the soft blue eyes; and as Grimalkin trotted round to his left side, the absent tip of his left arm, the grey shirt discreetly pinned back over its stump.

"How sad," said Eilidh, her breath seeming to labour. "That there is no mention, from our good Lord, about our beloved beasties and Grimalkin joining us in the afterlife. I shall see my darling Alfie, I doubt not that. But our wee fluffy pals ... Always so noble! Always so loyal. With us through so much."

"Ooooh," said the man. "Ooo, I dunny know about that. Who's tae say? Our good Lord had a place for each of the beasties on the ark."

"That wee cat," said Eilidh, unhearing. "There was something about him. Something ... different about him."

The man smiled again with a bow of the head. From downstairs there came the sing of the kettle on the hob.

"I'll just nip down and get us a tea. Would you like that, Eilidh, darling?"

"Uh-huh. Tea," said Eilidh.

The man lifted his chair back across the floor. With gnarled hands he gripped a tray of cups and saucers, and made his way carefully out the door, holding down the top of each cup with a thumb to stop them jingling.

In the new silence, a peculiar happiness flooded over the old cat. Here he was watching his closest human friend die, and yet he felt an unexpected glow developing between him and the woman in front of him as if he were somehow closer to her now than ever before. From outside, the wind swirled, making the wisteria tremble against the windowpanes.

Then, to his astonishment, Grimalkin felt a hand reach out and come to rest upon his head. A little tickle followed, before the hand moved perfectly along the contours of his back in a big stroke, continuing along his tail and even making a little up-turn at its end where it had once been crooked.

"Mah wee moggy. Is that you?"

Eilidh's eyes remained latched to the ceiling above, but her mouth had formed into a gentle smile. "I ken yer here wie me! Thank ye for coming. Can we pass the days together anon, Moggie?"

Grimalkin sank to his belly and curled into Eilidh's side, feeling her deep warmth envelop him.

Several minutes passed. A robin sang, its flock of looping crotchets ducking under the half-open window. Downstairs, the cups clinked against the sink as the kettle ceased its whistling. The cries of the revellers fell quiet and the wind dropped to a whispering breeze.

Unaware. All so unaware.

Finally, some minutes later, there was that last flicker of sunlight on the floorboards, one last gust of wind, a last scuffle of footsteps and the last chime of birdsong that coincided with Eilidh MacNeil's time on this earth. And all the spirit, passion and longing that accompanied her body on this mortal coil slipped away and were no more.

Grimalkin's Observations

Decoration:	Oddly shabby.
Humans:	Everyone seems hungry.
Technology:	Suspicious food colourings.
Monarch:	Queen Elizabeth II.

Fifth Haunting,
July 1969

VROOOOOOM.

Grimalkin stirred.

Vrrrrr . . . rroooooooom.

There, in front of him, was the devil incarnate. *In machine form.*

Vrooooooooooooooooooooooooooom!

Without a moment's thought, Grimalkin scrambled up the side of a bow-fronted wardrobe like a lizard, eyes as wide as tennis balls, and his fur frizzed up, making him twice his usual size. He could see the whole room up here, though he immediately began to question whether he could ever make it back down again.

He was in the front bedroom, the one with the two parallel windows. The noise of the devil-machine ricocheted between the walls like a tossed hammer, making the whole room into a heinous cage of noise.

A little dish rested on a bedside table with a wedge of cake on it, and a young man pushed the machine by its great long tail. At least, Grimalkin assumed he was a man as he had a beard, though he also sported hair so long and blonde it resembled a horse's tail, swishing left and right over his shoulders as he moved the machine around. It was only then that Grimalkin noticed: the devil-machine appeared to be eating crumbs off the carpet.

Grimalkin reared up as the devil-machine approached the wardrobe, letting out a long hiss, even though it was several feet beneath his wardrobe-top perch.

Mercy, mercy! Hellish instrument of death, reveal thy purpose or begone!

The machine continued its infernal scorched-earth domination of the rug, lapping up more and more crumbs like some confounded robotic boar.

The end has come! Grimalkin thought, tremoring on the wardrobe, his eyes glued to the progress of the devil-machine like a theatre-goer's binoculars on a Covent Garden prima donna. *Has the restless union betwixt human and cat finally engineered machines of feline torture? I want none of it! Bring me death! Gracious, sweet, silent death!*

The young man stamped violently on the side of the machine. Suddenly, its heinous roar subsided. The man left the room, his back arched and his hair sloshing lankly around a vibrant red shirt.

Slowly, gradually, Grimalkin's pupils narrowed, his fur de-spiking and his whiskers once more projecting out at right angles to his face.

You would have me think you dead, beast, but I will not be so foolish. You and I shall always be at war, FIE FIE!

Keeping his gaze fixed on the devil-machine, Grimalkin flopped his form down the side of the wardrobe, allowing himself to land clumsily on a nearby chair. From there he inched onto the rug, belly to the floor, creeping ever closer to the masterpiece of war itself, which now stood suspiciously silent, its tail projected upright into the air.

Speak, coward, and reveal what you are!

He inched round to the front, where heat emanated from a recently extinguished lightbulb on the machine's front. A large bag was clipped against the beast's skeleton, in which it no doubt stored the carcasses of its prey. On its crumb-eating underside, two huge brushes lay deathly still, above which its brain rose in a grey dome.

Never one to be cowed by a usurper to his space, Grimalkin jabbed the beast with his paws.

Fie, speak if you be brave, villain of Lucifer!

Of course, his paws just slid through the beast, but it made him feel somewhat satisfied. Nothing. The machine sat quite silent.

His confidence gradually rising, Grimalkin stood on the domed brain of the machine. It was warm under his paws; no

133

doubt the business of villainy had left the beast feeling exhausted. Perhaps it was now dead? *Aye, perhaps it has perished!* Only then did he notice another tail emanating from the machine – a wire – which he followed with his eyes until it disappeared off beside the wardrobe where it lay embedded into the wall.

Electricity! I knew it. That Edwardian Mr Barrie was right in 1909 – it really is the work of the Devil!

The closest thing Grimalkin had seen to the beast was a Victorian bellows which Eilidh had often used to get the fires going on mizzle-ridden winter mornings when the wood had got damp if another servant had left the lid off the garden log store.

"Mum ... Mum ... Muuuuuum!?" Grimalkin spied the young man down the hall yelling into the kitchen, where music was playing loudly.

Mum? What is a "mum"? It's ma'am as in "ham", you foolish boy, thought Grimalkin.

"Mum, I've done the bedroom."

A sharp, ricocheting voice returned from the kitchen. "Eh, no! Have ye done the living room flairs, too?"

"Aye ... "

"And ye've tidied the box room fir the new lodger, aye?"

"Aye ... "

"And put the scran fae Ingin Johnny[1] in the press?

---

[1] A phrase for much-loved old Edinburgh onion sellers, and seasonal migrants, who brought onions over from Brittany each year. They were known as affable and would often stop by for a coffee and, in the case of 7/7 Marchmont Crescent, some suet pudding and a scratch of Grimalkin's ear.

"Aye ..."

"Jeezo, can ye talk to me in more than one syllable, ye morose laddie?"

What in tarnation are they saying to each other? thought Grimalkin, his head spinning with these odd new phrases. He padded down the hallway, turning left into the kitchen, where the young man was leaning against the door to the pantry, his hair falling lankly over his shirt, which appeared to have no buttons and short sleeves. His mother was at the sink – the exact same sink Eilidh had washed at in 1895 – swirling round some grey water from a recent wash. She was a squat, dumpy little lady, who seemed to move in bursts like a fieldmouse. But the most extraordinary thing about her was her hair – it looped high above her head into two marmalade-coloured wheels that wobbled as she scurried about like a wind-beaten gorse bush. The hair almost looked like it had a life of its own, and something about the two parallel loops that drew back into a slanted-back peak reminded Grimalkin of the hind legs of a grasshopper.

"You're nay tae get pished again, John, de ye understand?"

"Pished"? What is "pished"? mused Grimalkin, gazing at the woman archly.

"Not wie the new lodger moving in. We need that cash. I dinnae want them thinking they've moved in tae some jakie doss house."

The young man knitted his brows, which were just visible behind his curtain of hair. He skulked out the room. Grimalkin followed him to the back bedroom, from whence a loud racket blared unpleasantly. Following him in, Grimalkin was shocked to find that the "racket" was in fact emanating from a spinning record and so must in fact be "music". Strange pieces of art lined the wall, but rather than exist in appropriate gilt frames to set the oils off respectfully on the canvas, these "paintings" – if they were such a thing – didn't have frames at all; they appeared to be just sheets of paper, tacked up in the most unbecoming and scruffy way.

One of them said "Make Love Not War" in frighteningly bold letters, and another (which must've been installed when the young man was inebriated for it was positioned at an angle) bore the words "The Beatles" next to four men who seemed to exist inside a sort of melting rainbow of colour.

My, my, either this man is as mad as hops or the future has finally arrived, pondered Grimalkin, who had never before seen these colours placed together. The swirling blues and yellows and reds almost had a trance-like effect on his brain, making him feel giddy and oddly joyous.

The young man plonked onto his bed, rolling onto his side, like a sausage, his hair flowing up the pillow like a Renaissance muse (though something told Grimalkin this particular man would not have appreciated this comparison). The well-travelled cat was beginning to wonder whether the man had just received some terrible news or felt queer about the stomach. Alas, these concerns were allayed as the man leaned over to his bedside table and lowered the bar onto a large flat disk. The crackle of the needle running across the disk made Grimalkin close his eyes blissfully, just as the man began to do the same.

Music surged into the room at double volume . . . Music that was so intoxicating, unusual and catchy that Grimalkin hardly had the chance to feel annoyed by its unnecessary loudness. In fact, Grimalkin was quite unable to process this new music; it felt like it was coming from another world – an exciting vibrant realm where everyone dances and parties and wears colourful clothes. Such an unexpected combination of notes, and timbres! So upbeat and lively and . . . *strange*. It made Handel's "Messiah", once played on Mr Calvert's gramophone, in this very room on Sunday mornings, seem positively bland.

But what on earth is a "yellow submarine"? That is what I wish to know.

The man kicked off his white shoes, letting them fall to the floor with a clonk as he beat his hands mid-air as if playing an invisible drumkit suspended above his bed.

Grimalkin found himself buoyed. Something about this strange song and its repeating beats had the same psychedelic effect on his ears that the colourful pictures had had on his eyes. He began to feel his judgemental inner voice grow quiet . . .

Wooooah. This age is strangely . . . nourishing! Why, the other decades seem positively black and white compared to this decade! I have never beheld such levity of spirit!

137

"John, Jooooohn . . ." came a voice from the kitchen, where a second wireless was now blaring out in competition. "Have you fed the cat, John? She's gittin' around my ankles."

"Nooooo, I'm gunnae soon," said John, who Grimalkin was beginning to think spoke more through his nose than his mouth.

"Well, do it, please, before you go out, she's prowlin' about ma legs."

John rose slowly as if in great arthritic pain and moped to the door before pulling open a drawer in the hall.

"Ppprrrr-oaw." A little kitten came running over the carpeted floor, craning its neck to John as he lifted a tin sullenly out of a drawer. He upturned its contents into a bowl from which the kitten lapped voraciously. A peculiar, synthetic meaty smell swirled in Grimalkin's direction. It was an odd smell, as if the fish guts, offal and pork pie meals of old had been all mixed together and tinned in a cylinder of gloop. It smelt delicious but also . . . *wrong*. Grimalkin meandered over to gaze at the kitten, who devoured the food as if it was her last meal on earth. Then he spied the tin, which had been left discarded. A strange band of writing swept around its side, like a poem. Grimalkin began to read:

The new Jellymeat Whiskas cat formula is chock-full of chunky meat and liver. With added Thiamin, it is the perfect source of nourishment for your furry friend. No wonder they fancy it – they know what's best for them!

Well, of all the patronising, lily-livered drivel. They are making tinned food now specially for cats? Mucky, chunky, processed victual. Human food is too good for us now, I suppose? And if you're going to insist on being affected, attend to your spelling: it's whiskERS, for heaven's sake, not whiskAS!

The cat food moment had slightly readjusted Grimalkin's feelings towards the age. Those inner Victorian beliefs and attitudes that had guided his thinking for so long did not die so easily, it turns out. He recalled having arrived in the 1940s and how frenetic and dramatic that had seemed, with the war and the bomb shelters ... This, by contrast, seemed to be an age of peace. And yet somehow, he felt more alienated among this era of psychedelic colours and strange hairdos than he did among a group of humans sheltering from bombs in an underground shelter. This age seemed to be gripped in an entirely artificial type of drama – a heady, over-the-top gaudiness of man, machine and hairstyle.

This is the last of my three straying lives. Heaven forfend, I suppose I must venture outside.

The young man, John, appeared to be getting ready for something. Slouching in front of a mirror, he was applying some peculiar balm to his hair, which he then pulled back in long glossy tendrils, tying it in a knot. From the wardrobe (also plastered in images) he extracted a white jacket, which he proceeded to pull himself into awkwardly, as if he refused to admit it was several sizes too small for him. Something about the procedure made Grimalkin think of a snake, trying to re-inhabit its old skin.

"Ye fed the cat, John, aye?"

"God, Mum, yessss . . ." hissed John, who was now stuffing cigarettes into his pocket.

"What time you back? I'm nay leaving the door on the latch again, not aifter last time."

"I'm staying at Elaine's," said John.

"Oh aye? And what do her parents think about that? My day she wouldnae be allowed out with yous, let alone stay over."

"Well, it's not your day, is it, Mum. It's 1969. We've got the Beatles and the Space Race. You had wars and . . . the *Titanic.*"

"I beg your pardon, I am not *that* old, young man," said the woman. She entered the room, grinding her cigarette end into an ashtray she had cupped in her left hand. She looked the boy up and down quizzically. "And all this carry-on for men on the moon? I'll believe it when I see it."

John upturned a bottle of something into the palm of his hand before patting his cheeks with a *slap-slap-slap.* A nauseating smell of roses and ginger swirled round Grimalkin's nostrils. "See you later."

But he hasn't put a tie on, thought Grimalkin, his eyes pinching. *Wait, sir, you mustn't leave without a tie on, you will be jeered at!*

John headed down the hallway, which had been painted white and sported a long stretch of cabinetry covered in an array of little figurines made of china. He was heading out and Grimalkin knew this would be the last opportunity he would have to see beautiful Edinburgh – the Edinburgh of the future in all its bulbous-hairdo'd, crazy-coloured, robotic glory.

* * *

On the street outside, Grimalkin peered over at John, who leaned against a lamp post, his right leg bent and the sole of his shoe pressed flat against its wrought-iron base. It was the same lamp post Grimalkin had seen being lit in the 1890s, when it was still fuelled by oil, and then in the 1910s, when it ran on gas, and then again in 1953, when it was wrapped in coronation buntings. Today, it looked especially sturdy and proud. It had seen so much; entire lives had risen and been snuffed out under its timeless orange glow. Grimalkin felt a sudden pang of sadness. That lonely feeling that had accompanied him so often during his hauntings returned with a vengeance. It was only among these things – these inanimate objects that stood year in year out – that Grimalkin could find any real consistency and comfort. This venerable old post of steel, endlessly illuminating the night air, had been like a gentleman keeping watch at his window for an incoming storm.

Humph, kindship with a lamp, thought Grimalkin, feeling a little bit pathetic. *There's something I never thought I'd feel.* John

lit a cigarette and sent its smoke curling up through the fili-
greed glass lantern. To suffer in silence is one thing, but to *feel*
in silence ... To miss and crave and love in silence ... These
were emotions that would rend the heart of any living being.
Right now, Grimalkin once again felt an overwhelming need
to reach out across the ages and feel the touch of another
human. That sweep of a hand across the fur. That tickle behind
the ear. Like this lamp post, he had seen it all ... He had seen
every last thing yet was condemned to never speak or feel.

*Will I ever touch again? How will all this end? Cat-sìth, tell
me, how will all this end?*

All of a sudden, a tiny motorcar, no bigger than a coal
bin, came careening down the road, pulling to a sudden stop
right beside John. A young lady's face emerged from the
passenger-side window. Her hair clung flatly to her scalp,
and her blouse flashed in vivid stripes along with her eyes,
which seemed mischievous.

"Alright, mate?"

"Alright, mate"? winced Grimalkin, *What is an "Alright, mate"?*

"You got the gear, John Boy?" enquired the girl.

"Aye, in mah pocket, hen. All groovy," John replied with a
cheeky smile.

"Nice," said the girl with a click of her mouth. "Far-out
shirt, by the way, John Boy, I like it."

John smiled, bowing his head down to the passenger-side
window. "Alright, driver, top shades, mah man. We ready to
party?"

The car's driver wore big dark sunglasses with lenses so dark you couldn't see his eyes through them. He sported a thin moustache that curved down at the sides, and a morose expression that looked like it had been chiselled into his face with a flint blade. His stubborn glumness was a direct contrast to his clothes, which were dazzlingly bright, and consisted of orange and green trousers, and a shirt so floral it made Grimalkin question whether he had recently been out frolicking in a physic garden.

John craned his head further, looking into the car's rear seat. "Ah, Logan's here, too, eh? Good to know we're going to get some intellectual conservation on this auspicious day."

"Awright, John, mate, how's tricks," intoned a man on the back seat clutching a bottle Grimalkin knew immediately must contain some kind of alcohol.

So "Alright, mate" must be their acknowledgement of each other in this age, considered Grimalkin. *The equivalent of a doff of the cap? Whatever happened to "good day" or "Hullo"! Alright, mate indeed!*

John pushed himself off the lamp post with his foot and ambled over to the car, stamping out his cigarette with a turn of his shoe heel. His sulking way of moving with a curved back and dragging feet had suddenly evolved into a kind of indolent swagger at the sight of the girl's smiling face in the car's window frame. As John approached, she met his gaze and held it as she opened the door and eased her way out of the car. She then swung the seat forward, and John got into

143

the back alongside Logan, who shifted his alcohol bottle in a cackhanded way, spilling some on the seat.

He's squiffy! That gentleman in the back is squiffy, I put my name to it! thought Grimalkin with a judgemental pinch of the eyes.

But there was something else that shocked Grimalkin and made him rear up slightly on his paws. As a Victorian cat, he had fairly set views on human vestment, particularly among the females of that species. For instance, a lady's dress, particularly in Edinburgh, should *always* include a petticoat in case the North Sea wind should gust suddenly and put her undergarments in a state of exposure. It went without saying. That way, one could perambulate safe in the knowledge the nether regions were always shielded from view. Grimalkin simply could never comfortably envision it any other way.

Yet today, as the girl got out of the car, Grimalkin was quite sure he had received an unintended snapshot of the lady's ... *undergarments!* Her skirt was so short and high it seemed to Grimalkin more to resemble a gentleman's belt or cummerbund.

I say, this is most saucy, mused Grimalkin at the pavement's edge, as the girl squeezed back into the car. *Why, if she isn't a coquette about to parade the town? I dare say no cat or human was meant to behold what I did just ... behold. And I thought John naked for neglecting to wear a tie. Saints preserve me.*

"Get a move on, Elaine, an' gieza scush of yer Sprite," said the driver.

Elaine still had one leg out of the car, her bag on the pavement, with the car's fumes now adding a bluish haze to the air. A daring thought crossed Grimalkin's mind. What if he jumped in the car? Cat-sìth had not mentioned what would happen if he reached the end of a life and fell asleep in a peculiar location ... On a turret atop Edinburgh Castle, for instance, or on a boat on the North Sea. Would Cat-sìth still return him to his usual slumberous repose at 7/7 Marchmont Crescent for the beginning of the next age?

Three he strays ... Oh, drat it, in for a penny, in for a pound! thought Grimalkin, hopping up onto Elaine's lap as she slammed the door.

The inside of the car was dizzying. Music blared, coloured stickers and pictures studded the wheel and front dashboard in a chaotic manner and an odd herby smell filled the air that made Grimalkin feel somewhat swimmy about the head. A rumbling sound throbbed up through the car's seats as it sped off over the cobbles, taking turns far too quickly. Even as a ghost cat endowed with the powers of invisibility, Grimalkin was still not invulnerable to the laws of movement. Scents poured through the window, some familiar and some alien – the creamy whiff of the Murchie's Dairy in Tollcross ... The heady whiff of some kind of bathroom unguent.[2] He steadied

---

[2] Grimalkin was most likely smelling the J. & G. Cox glue and gelatine factory on Gorgie Road.

himself on his paws as famous Edinburgh landmarks rushed passed – the Meadows, the old hospital on Lauriston Place, the Doctors Bar on Forrest Road, which appeared to be doing a good trade in 1969, its walls and outdoor seats lined with smoking louche men and women, much like Elaine and John. Now the car was leaving the extremities of Southside Edinburgh ... The outposts of what Grimalkin knew from his perusal of Mr Calvert's maps. They hurtled past the Flodden Wall and the Greyfriars Kirkyard, and along George IV bridge, its high-sided buildings black and caked with coal soot. Turning right, the car trundled down the Royal Mile and its long strip of tightly packed tenements, known to Grimalkin by the huge edifice of St Giles' Cathedral, seen on so many postcards and newspapers, its ribbed turret-like hand clutching at the sky.

What the veritable dazes, seethed Grimalkin, beginning to feel sick at the speed. *Whatever happened to good old-fashioned restraint and decorum? There's no necessity for this pace. These people are adults, are they not?*

A song blurted out of the automobile's radiogram. The present party of travelling revellers started singing and waving their coloured sleeves in the air.

"Here, mate," piped up a voice beside Grimalkin on the back seat. "I always thought that lyric was *fly me to Dunoon* ... ken the place in Argyll."

"It's *the moon,* Logan, you utter prized numpty," said Elaine.

The car exploded into uncontrollable yelps of laughter. *What on earth is a "numpty"?* thought Grimalkin.

Elaine spun round to the back seats, her pretty eyes beaming wide. "You honestly thought the words were 'fly me to Dunoon'?"

"Aye, is that no what it is? Fly me to . . . Dunoon. I swear it's Dunoon, man, yous are all talking mince."

"It's 'the moooooon'," cried the car in unison.

"Oh, right, fine, groovy," replied Logan lazily. "Ah stand corrected."

"Aye, the *moon*," said Elaine. "Ken, the thing we're going to Calton Hill for? To see the men landing on it?"

"Ah thought we were going to Dunoon!" said Logan. He leaned forward and turned to the driver conspiratorially, spilling yet more of his bottle of drink. "Ah we no going to Dunoon?"

"Nooooo!" said the car in unison between bursts of laughter.

"He's pished already," said Elaine, turning to the driver with a grin. She pulled out a pack of cigarettes from a bulbous handbag.

The car took a sharp left down a slope before stopping suddenly. Grimalkin steadied himself on the car's chilly metal frame. He could just about crane his neck up to the window line. They appeared to be in Waverley, Edinburgh's principal railway station. Grimalkin had never visited, of course, but had heard of the famous station that nestled in the gorge to the north of the Royal Mile, where there once stood a

147

putrefied loch used for the ducking of witches. It was a forbidding and noisy space, the sort of environment that no cat would enter voluntarily. From his position in the squat rear seat, Grimalkin could only see the far wall and glass ceiling, which was buckled up into peaks at intervals, and was caked in thick black grime, blocking out all daylight. A constant bone-shaking rumbling tremored through the ground and up into Grimalkin's paws via the car's frame. Through the smear-streaked ceiling glass, Grimalkin could just spy the great clock face of the North British Hotel, which famously was always five minutes fast so travellers would not miss their trains as they hurried along North Bridge and Princes Street.

Alright, mate, this all seems rather unpleasant. May we leave now, please?

Grimalkin was familiar with trains – these long snake-like noisy things used to transport humans; though he was pleased he'd never had to travel on one. Often, on hot summer evenings in the 1890s, he would hear the local services chuffing up from Morningside, just a mile or so from the foot of Kilgraston Road, their whistles echoing through gaps in the tenements. Hearing them some way off was fine. They posed no threat. Once, however, he had spied one on a trip to the vet in Blackford Hill, which was located next to the railway line. He had looked in horror and awe as a train snivelled into view in the cutting behind the veterinary practice, "WAVERLEY" displayed proudly on the machine's brow, as the train and its carriages rolled past in a hair-raising din of metal upon metal, thick clouds of smoke billowing up to the window. It had felt almost alive – a great jagged horizon of fizzing brass pipes and jet-black domes, of enormous steel rods on the wheels that paddled frantically in a blur. It was terrifying.

"He's coming into platform five," said the driver.

Elaine flung open her door. Resting his paws on the armrest, Grimalkin was able to raise himself to the car's rear window and offer himself a better view.

My, my, what a lot of hurrying numpties!

The sight that greeted his eyes was both alarming and mesmerising. Men and women in a welter of colour whizzed back and forth across the station concourse. Many of the women were wearing short skirts, just like Elaine, which made Grimalkin regret his early decision in considering her a coquette. It was clearly a fashion of the times, just like the open-topped shirts, vibrant oranges, yellows and zigzag stripes. But at the same time, Grimalkin couldn't help but notice that much of the surroundings did still bear the stamp of Queen Victoria's day: the station's great arching roof, its railings, and handsome clock hanging from the iron trusswork above, all bore the filigreed swirly style of the late monarch. *And may she live forever!* thought Grimalkin involuntarily. Even the railway carriages that lined the long platforms, silent and brooding, and the stout, behatted porters who hauled luggage off and on, looked like what Grimalkin could recall from the 1890s.

What *was* different, however, and almost as alarming as the short skirts, was the train itself. Grimalkin had never beheld such a grotesque abomination of steel and metal! It made the devil carpet cleaner machine look positively benign! Rather than a pulsating mass of brass pipes and pistons, this . . . "train" . . . was a mere green lozenge with two symmetrical snub noses at the front and back. Instead of producing majestic gouts of steam, a smeary chimney choked out a sort of bluish-coloured clag, as if the tar from its innards – for surely it did run on tar? – had emulsified and been chucked out in a vomit. A yellow strip ran along its bottom with a nameplate that said "THE ELIZABETHAN" beneath a frightening symbol that looked like the letter "Z" crossing two lines.

"What-cha, Keithy, over here," said Elaine amid the deafening rumble of the idling train.

A tall man with a prominent chin and leather jacket strode through the crowd. He could have been any age, but from his slicked-back hair, which receded at the temples, Grimalkin sensed he might be a little older than the rest of the party. As he approached, Grimalkin noticed that his eyes were jet black and beady, much like a bear's, and nestled deep in his head, making it difficult to discern what he was looking at. Accompanying him, like a tsunami, was a strong stench of alcohol and the rather-too-easy manner of a human who thinks himself more attractive than he really is. Something about this, and the way he shouldered his path through the crowd, made Grimalkin take an immediate dislike to Keith. His top teeth protruded at jagged angles, like a line of tombstones, and when he smiled his eyes became even beadier and his chin even sharper. As he neared, Grimalkin noticed that the fingers of his left hand were curled around a small cube, with an antenna – presumably some kind of radiogram. The fingers on that hand were strangely delicate, almost effeminate, and protruded into long talon-like nails which were rinded underneath with black. Before he was free of the crowds, Elaine ran over to hug him. Such an unseemly display of public affection Grimalkin had never before beheld.

Why not show some restraint, you swooning pair? thought Grimalkin.

Keith got in the front seat of the car.

"Groovy, I'll see you guys up the hill," said Elaine, peering into the crowded car.

"You can sit on my lap, dolly babe," said Keith, with a sideward glance up at Elaine. He spoke nasally in a northern English accent, which rather took Grimalkin by surprise.

"You numpty, how can I sit there?"

"Yeah, you canny fit there," piped up John from the back seat, a little pathetically.

"Oooh, come on!" Keith rubbed his hand around Elaine's waist. "Show us a bit of sugar." Quick as a flash, he had crooked his hand around Elaine and pulled her onto his lap, closing the door with his left hand. Elaine let out a shriek.

"Nuff's enough, play nice, guys. How's tricks, Keithy?" said the driver, starting the engine and launching the tiny car hurtling up the ramp of Waverley station, its passengers jostling in unison, like one single enormous animal. Grimalkin eyed Keith's oddly effeminate hands as his long, spiny fingers twisted the dial on the portable radiogram, his other hand resting on Elaine's lap. On the back seat, newly sullen and gazing glumly out of the window, John seemed to have slunk into himself at the arrival of Keith.

A crackle amplified and from the radiogram came an American voice.

"Altitude 4200. Houston, you're go for the landing. Over. Roger, understand. Go for landing 3000 feet, copy."

"Come on, driver," cried Keith, "put your foot down, mate. It's about to happen and we're packed like sardines on Waterloo Place. Fuck's sake!"

The car whipped nimbly between a bus and the pavement before scooting up the slope to Calton Hill. Suddenly, all of central Edinburgh panned up before Grimalkin's eyes – that perfect, timeless view ... The castle like a cork on top of the ancient hill, the clock of the North British Hotel gallantly crowning the east end of Princes Street. He knew this existed ... He knew this scene was here at the time of his birth; these fine, proud buildings and these vivid, tumultuous, drama-laden skies like great stage backdrops. All this architecture ... knitting together the human and the natural in one vista: the sea to the right and Arthur's

Seat to the left; the timeless view over Edinburgh from Calton Hill.

"Altitude velocity down nicely. Two hundred feet, four and a half down, five and a half down."

"Come oaahn, man. I need a slash, gonnae just stop here, mate," said Logan from the back seat.

"Will here do alright, guys?" said the driver, spinning the wheel of the little car towards the verge.

"How's tricks", "Awright, mate", "groovy", "numpties", thought Grimalkin, his head spinning and feeling a little disgusted. *Why have I missed one? What an unseemly tongue this age converses in! Has the great English language we knew and loved from Shakespeare and Milton withered and died?* His irritation had made him squirm and consequently slip down into the car's footwell, where he was getting closely acquainted with Elaine's chunky-heeled flower-print boots.

The car shuddered to a stop. As the driver-side door latch undid, the car's passengers practically burst onto the grass verge, like a de-corked champagne bottle. Grimalkin blinked. The grass beneath his feet felt hot and wiry and was smattered with little pieces of scraps – the odd delicious-smelling sausage or piece of bread. All about him, people teemed and frolicked. A huge speaker blasted music in one corner, and at another, people were forming a disorderly queue to purchase moon-themed souvenirs, the brightness of their clothes reminding Grimalkin of a sun-drenched puddle shortly after rainfall. There were people on each other's shoulders, people smoking cigarettes in little huddles with open-topped shirts and sleeveless blouses. There were people with radiograms strapped to their ears, and others waving placards depicting a particularly handsome, white-toothed human in great love-hearts under the straplines "Love USA!" and "Never Forgotten!"[3] and others who were clearly inebriated, a little way off, dancing in circles like druids. Children ran between the crowds like mice, some dressed with peculiar metal hats, fashioned out of tinfoil, and others seemingly the moon themselves . . . ensconced in large crescent-shaped pieces of board. *Wild abandon*, Grimalkin kept thinking. *I have never beheld such wild abandon!*

"Okay, guys, guys . . . " said Elaine, twiddling the volume on the radio. "Oi, Logan, shut your gob and listen up!"

"Houston, Tranquillity Base here. The Eagle has landed."

A cheer went up, unlike a cheer Grimalkin had ever heard from humans before. Champagne bottles popped and people leaped and reeled. The party Grimalkin had arrived with in the car fell into an embrace. (Grimalkin saw Keith's hand snake down Elaine's back to her skirt, and Elaine promptly repositioning it upon her waist.) The whole caterwauling was bewildering and exhausting and, while Grimalkin could

---

[3] No doubt JFK, assassinated six years earlier in 1963. Though it should be noted that the tinfoil hat wearers wore similar shirts, but with the face crossed out, and alongside the more outré slogan "It's All Fake! They're Reprogramming Your Minds!!"

appreciate the momentousness of a human on the moon, he found himself frightened by the crazed revelry of the humans around him. It was as if they were all tuned in to a mode of existence that he – as a cat – would never ever understand.

A little way off, behind a small knot of gorse and shrub, a huddle of people had joined hands in a circle. *What is happening over here looks far groovier*, thought Grimalkin, trotting over. Approaching, he realised they were a troupe of devoted Christians, and were murmuring a group prayer in front of a crucifix that had been placed on a little wooden plinth in the centre of the circle.

"May the Lord Almighty seek mercy on the souls of those who seek for higher causes than Him, for He alone is the Truth and the Light. Amen . . . May He take the souls of these sinners and return them to safety and forgive them for their fraternisation in causes higher than the Lord Almighty. Amen!"

The sight of these defectors made Grimalkin feel oddly calm. *There still are believers*, he thought. *The humans still have a need for a higher force in God!*

"May the Lord guide us in His perfect image and let us seek no image but His. Amen."

Quite right, thought Grimalkin. *Quite right, very good, yes.*

Then, like all cats who have had too much stimulation and excitement, Grimalkin felt a delicious wave of tiredness fall over him. The din from the singing revellers quietened, and the crinkle of tinfoil on the hats of costumed revellers softened into a whisper. He lay down in the grass and rolled over, showing his belly to the sun and letting the North Sea breeze flick his whiskers to and fro. *I am fatigued of this age. Too many numpties. It is too much.*

And with that, he lost grasp of his thoughts and dropped into sleep.

Grimalkin's Observations

Decoration: Flowery wallpaper (horrendous).
Humans: Inebriated numpties in tinfoil hats.
Technology: Portable radiogram.
Monarch: Queen Elizabeth II.

Sixth Haunting,
October 1997

"*THE BIG BREAKFAST* COMES TO Channel 4 in an hour, but before that a hop across the Pond to the sitcom everyone's talking about. What will Rachel say? It's *Friends*."

Oh, give a cat some peace!

Grimalkin opened one eye. In front of him was a television. On it were a series of coloured umbrellas spinning around and a group of men and women jumping into a water fountain and getting very wet indeed.

God, what cursed age of hedonism and numpties must I endure now?! Death, I should've chosen death!

Grimalkin's head was pounding as his right ear flicked involuntarily to the upbeat theme tune which blared out from the television's speakers. *Oh, sweet death. Come to me!*

In an attempt to take his mind off the irritating theme tune, Grimalkin cast his mind back. It was all a bit of a blur.

The last thing he could remember was falling asleep with a coven of witches on a lawn on Calton Hill. Or were they witches? Wasn't a druid there too? And sheep? And everyone was dancing and spinning over something. Fragments of memory and thought eddied around Grimalkin's brain like leaves twisting in a gust.

The moon, was it not? They had all been going to celebrate a human on the moon?

The twanging music weaved into people talking in an American accent. Grimalkin had still not opened his right eye. His tummy lurched in that now-familiar time-travelling motion sickness ... *Gosh, I feel queer. Queer and heady ... and rum about the tum.*

His mind moved to Eilidh and he remembered with a sudden stab of pain that she was dead. Gone. Somehow, his haunting of 1969 had been so crazy, so blisteringly quick and lurchingly dramatic, that he was sure he hadn't thought about Eilidh barely once. This made him feel guilty, as if he had betrayed her memory in 1969. Now, all the memories of Eilidh's loss and her death came flooding back with abandon as his head winced from the infernal happy-clappy music from the television. He found himself once again regretting his decision to sample the ages and thought longingly of the delicious endless sleep of death – the only oblivion from which we can be assured we are *never* awoken from by inane musical compositions.

Now on the television, the humans that were previously frolicking in the fountain were all sitting on a sofa in a café.

Grimalkin swivelled his head left and right, finding himself located in the fire grate, which was dusty and cold with a strong draught racing down the chimney breast and ruffling his fur. Outside, the sky was clay-white, with no shape – the sort of sky that Grimalkin knew, from Victorian times, would often set the humans scurrying around with worried looks, and stating such comments as *"gonnae snow the night"* or *"fetch in the geese, for there'll be a hoarfrost the morn . . . "*

He turned his head into the room. Of all the faddish incarnations of style and design inflicted upon this grand Victorian room, *this* age was sure to be the worst. The first thing that took his attention was a huge dangling globe – or was it meant to be a lampshade? – hanging in the middle of the room. It dangled from the same spot where the chandelier used to elegantly crown the room and could only be described as a great paper balloon with a lightbulb in the centre. The walls themselves were bare and pockmarked, as if many generations of pictures had been attached there, then wrenched off months later, only to be reattached again. An overloaded bookshelf next to the door had started to slant, flirting with collapse, and beside it a bed extended into the room, from the inside wall, long and thin with no frame, like a sacrificial plinth.

They have made the lounge into a bed chamber?! thought Grimalkin, taking in the space. *What a silly notion! This is the lounge. Who in their rightful mind would sleep behind a bay window?*

159

But one thing was stranger and more offensive to the eye than all of these things. Along by the far wall, and covered in piles of blankets, was a purple sofa that appeared to be . . . filled with air!

Well, tweak my whiskers and call me Rita! thought Grimalkin, eyeing the monstrosity with rolls of further inflatable pieces for armrests and footstalls. *What on earth is the advantage of inflatable furniture? What else are they inflating in this age? The food? Their books . . . Each other?!* Grimalkin pawed over nervously and sniffed the sofa. It smelled like the sole of a boot, but with an odd synthetic tinge that he hadn't confronted before. *My, is it made of rubber? Its mere presence gives me the morbs. We have achieved the nadir of interior design!*

There was an odd mix of items scattered about the room, so much so that Grimalkin could barely discern its purpose. Pantry? Kitchen? Bedroom? Drawing room? Laundry store? As perhaps the untidiest room Grimalkin had ever beheld, he was beginning to think it must be *all* these things at once. But what was worse than this was that the room seemed entirely white: the walls were white, the woodwork and the ceiling were white, as were the coffee table, the bookshelf and the little table the television was standing on. White was everywhere, its blandifying glare burning into Grimalkin's eyes like acid.

Around the fireplace was a scattering of photographs – in *colour* no less – arranged in an arch above the hearth. A long-faced girl with arresting eyes and fox-red hair repeated throughout these pictures; sometimes on a boat, sometimes in

160

front of a campfire with friends; sometimes plummeting through the air connected to string. One even had her sitting astride a horse with her hands outstretched and her thumbs up. Clothes littered the floor in untidy piles; the last time Grimalkin had seen clothes piled thus was when the late Victorian master was awaiting Eilidh's arrival to take the laundry on a Sunday evening. There were some trousers made of a stitching that was familiar to Grimalkin from the 1960s, some socks, and a large jumper with a hood bearing the slogan '97 *Leavers Winchester College.* There was a herby, musty smell in the room, like mildew mixed with rosemary, and at the side of the bed dirty bowls lay piled next to cartons labelled Sunny Delight. Grimalkin sniffed one with a scummy residue – dried milk. It was enough to turn any self-respecting cat's stomach.

Suddenly, Grimalkin clenched his paws, his heart pounding. Unbeknownst to him, a girl had been lying on the purple inflatable sofa all this time. She had been camouflaged under a myriad blankets and cushions. She really must have been stock-still as even Grimalkin's ears – and they were sensitive ears – hadn't heard so much as a rustle. She was statuesque, her chest still and her eyes fixed vacantly on a television screen which flickered some distance away (the colourful-shirted humans still talking on the sofa of "Central Perk").

Is she stupefied? Has the purple inflated sofa stupefied her with its ugliness? Grimalkin peered round at her face which was white and drawn. *Gosh, she seems rather . . .*

161

The word "ill-bred" came to Grimalkin's mind, but he found himself shrinking from it. Time and experience were changing his views of people. The Victorian cat within him, with all its views on morality and people and life, was ebbing ever-slowly away. This girl's dishevelled appearance might once have prompted indignance in him ... even disgust. But across the decades, he had learned too much of the nuances of people's lives ... Too much of the misfortunes and struggles that humans suffer, unseen. He had witnessed the events that grew and shrank in the shadows, that tore them apart and shaped their characters and faces. He was growing less judgemental.

One thing was for sure – the girl on the inflated sofa was not the girl in the pictures around the fireplace; this girl was small, almost bird-like, with unwashed knotty hair and her legs canted up under her chin. Clutched in her hands was a cup held in the intense sort of way that a beggar might clasp a bowl under the nose of a passer-by. It was difficult to tell her age: she had a hunched and slightly pinched appearance that, in Grimalkin's experience, can make young humans look much older than their years. She was in a state that all species can recognise in themselves, and others. Whether cat, monkey, alligator or human ... it didn't matter; Grimalkin could detect the insidious presence of *this* state like a stubborn mould. Something about the pallor, the pelt's tautness, the watery, pinched look about the eyes. And so it was, that as Grimalkin eyed this lonely girl in this filthy room that his mind intoned, almost without thought: *she is hungry.*

162

Peptonised beef, that's what you require, my dear! thought Grimalkin. *Peptonised beef is still low cost in these parts, surely? Are Scotch oysters still not a penny from the Marchmont monger? Failing that, there's always offal.*

The girl wasn't wearing clothes, as such, but a sort of gown tied around her front by a cord in the style of a Chinese sage. Rather than being from gold-laced satin, this gown was grubby and red, except for the visage of a yellow teddy bear, with rounded ears, called "Winnie the Pooh".

Even now, after all the eras he'd haunted across, Grimalkin was still bemused by human attire. Having witnessed Elaine at the moon party in her short skirt exposing her knees, he thought he'd seen everything. But apparently not.

Is it ... a nightgown? thought Grimalkin, going in for a sniff. *Alas, no, it cannot be* (he looked at a clock that hung on the wall) *for it is 11.47 in the morn. No self-respecting human would enter their lounge at this hour in their nightwear, surely? It'd be profoundly un-groovy.*

Seconds later the lounge door opened slowly.

Who comes here? thought Grimalkin. *Another girl. Awright, mate?*

A tall woman emerged, resting her back importantly against the wall, her hand holding out the door from shutting. Grimalkin recognised her immediately as the girl in the photographs over the fireplace. There was a confident aloofness in the way she slowly manoeuvred herself into the room, letting the door close behind her. Everything about her stood in opposition with the girl on the settee, who seemed fragile and shrinking.

"Wazzup, Hannah," said the girl in a husky, deep voice.

Oh God, another abominable salutation. Grimalkin flinched.

"Oh, hi, Amelia," said Hannah, seeming a little shocked.

"Hannah, mate, seriously," continued the girl. As the door slammed shut, Grimalkin noted Hannah's eyes moving off to the side as if repulsed by the doorway girl's presence. She continued quietly sipping from her mug while watching television, which was now displaying the same people rabbiting away on *another* sofa, this time in a flat.

"Han? Mate? Not being funny, but can you, like, fuck off now? I need to plug in the modem?" said doorway girl. She seemed to end each sentence with an upturned inflexion of tone, as if everything was a question. It was a most peculiar, grating way of speaking that made Grimalkin curl his claws.

"Like you've been in here half the day?"

"But you only just said I could watch telly ten minutes ago?" said Hannah, whose voice sounded almost shrill in comparison to Amelia's drawl.

"Okay, whatever, but can you move now, yeah? You can't like, hog my bedroom, Hannah? We all have double bedrooms, yeah, that's why we pay the same? You can't say we're not being fair to you?"

"Okay. But you did say . . . " The girl on the sofa broke off as Amelia sighed and rolled her eyes. "Okay, okay, I'll go," whispered Hannah dejectedly.

Grimalkin lowered his belly to the floor and eyed the girl in the doorway archly. A contempt began to bubble and ferment inside of him. There was an expression on Amelia's face ... an expression that hid under the outward flickers of irritation. It was a sort of remote, disengaged look – a look which he had seen on various humans down the many ages he had haunted. It was, plain and simple, the countenance of privilege.

Hannah rose off the rubber sofa, which squeaked unpleasantly. She pressed a button on the television, making its picture shrink down into a little white hole.

Thank goodness for that, thought Grimalkin. *And what a ridiculous television chapter. Central Perk indeed. Humans just sitting around on a sofa talking in a cafeteria? It'll never last.*

Hannah placed the TV-controlling lozenge down, scurrying out the door like a cat who spies safety but needs to cross the path of a snarling dog in order to get there.

"Oh, and Han?" called Amelia, casting her head towards the door. "Have you seen my baccy?"

"No, sorry," replied Hannah weakly from the doorway.

"Oh, and Haaaaannnnahh?" yelled Amelia. "You going to English 1A later? Can you be an absolute legend and take some notes for me ... ?"

"Um, okay."

"Oh my God, like you are an *absolute lifesaver?* Thanks so much, you can use my bedroom anytime, 'kay, thanks, bye." She then turned to a broad-shouldered man in shorts and a red jersey, lolling against the doorframe to the adjacent bedroom. "I feel, like, totally guilty for making her move now?" said Amelia in a whisper, as the man laughed mutely beneath his tousled mop of hair.

Hmmmmmmmmmm, thought Grimalkin, leaping up onto a small coffee table. *I don't care for this Amelia dame and all her "wazzap" chat.* He settled his posterior on a pile of papers on the coffee table; a timeless pleasantry for any cat of any era. He gazed down idly to one particular sheet which bore a frightful headline in red ink: BRITISH GAS: FINAL WARNING FOR BILL UNDERPAYMENT. He turned again to look at Amelia as she entered the room, becoming suddenly transfixed by her piggy nose that upturned at the end in much the same way as her voice did at the end of sentences.

I'm beginning to get the measure of your nature, horsey girl, reflected Grimalkin. *And it is a most ungenial and disagreeable nature.*

Amelia sashayed on her stout ankles to the coffee table, turning on the TV before pulling up a foil packet labelled Monster Munch, Smokey Bacon from down the side of the sofa. Her eyes gawped at the television with the same séance-like transfixion as Hannah's had, moving only occasionally to pincer out a yellow starchy-looking snack from the Monster Munch packet.

What an age of slovenly idleness, Grimalkin considered. *It looks like they're positively bored of life . . . Bored of each other . . . Bored of the century!* He arched his head around the room once more, trying to piece together the components of this strange age. Only now did he notice that the mouldings and beautiful fairy cake cornicing around the living room ceiling (once the envy of all the houses on Marchmont Crescent) were dirty and cracked. Large stains bloomed across the ceiling where water had leaked down from the flat above, and the door itself had been stripped of its mouldings and boarded over with a large panel that bore the fearsome sign: FIRE DOOR: KEEP SHUT. The Edinburgh press[1] in the corner had also been boarded over, and painted the same white as the strange paper lampshade.

Suddenly the waft of the so-called Monster Munches caught Grimalkin's nose. It was to Grimalkin an odour of unspeakable majesty. From the moment it graced his nostrils he forgot all about the hideous decoration and his tummy began to murmur. Leaping off the coffee table, he climbed onto the settee next to Amelia. Here an exciting new bouquet of aromas reached his nose: peppered within the settee's folds was a smorgasbord of crumbs! The heady smell of chicken and fat and vinegar and bacon wafted up from the settee's countless ravines.

---

[1] An Edinburgh press is a recessed, door-shaped cupboard and shelving space often occupied by books, vases and sleeping cats. They are common across all Edinburgh tenement flats and were originally used by builders as an access point between flats at the time of their construction.

At that moment, a piece of Monster Munch tumbled from Amelia's mouth, and onto her lap. *What sweet culinary marvel is this Monster Munch? Fair Jehovah, let me sample this food of the Gods!*

Thinking little more of it (a cat's stomach overrides most other feelings), Grimalkin tiptoed across the sofa before raising himself up onto Amelia's lap.

Amelia leaped, as if stung by a nettle. Lurching forward, she looked left and right frantically, her nostrils flaring. Grimalkin felt a cold shiver as she passed right through his spectral form. A moment passed. Grimalkin remained quite still. Slowly, Amelia lowered her shoulders, the tension leaving her body. Her eyes resumed their fixation with the television screen.

Right-o, thought Grimalkin, *if I MAY be allowed to resume my snack I would be most grateful.*

He lowered his neck to the Monster Munch packet, positioning his left paw on the sofa for prime snack-grazing stability.

"Ahh, *fuuuuck!*"

Motion chaos. The Monster Munch packet launched into the air like a rocket. A glass of water smashed against a cereal bowl, sending it shattering to pieces. Grimalkin fled beneath the precarious bookcase, his tail spiked up like a witch's broom. Meanwhile, Amelia galloped around the room brushing herself frantically between shrieks.

"Woah, woah, woah, maaaate! What the hell?" The tall man with the tousled hair was standing in the doorway.

"Seriously, Rupert," panted Amelia, her eyes wide. "Something walked on me, I'm like not even joking? Like there's a mouse or something in here? It walked *over my lap!*"

"Oh, fucking hell, Amelia, you've burst the sofa, what the actual ... "

Grimalkin looked over at the purple sofa, which had sunk sorrowfully into the ground in a heap of cushions and rubber.

"I did *not* burst the sofa ... Something ... There was. Like SERIOUSLY, Rupert, something happened. Something was on me and brushed into my hand?"

Good, my claws are still up to muster, considered Grimalkin smugly, flexing his talons and admiring their sharpness.

The man rolled his eyes, turning out of the room to reveal the back of his jumper which read "Eton, 1995 Leavers" and a long list of names.

"And I've just flunked a level on Crash Bandicoot, thanks a LOT, mate."

"No, no, no, Rupert, I'm not even joking."

"Whatever."

"No, seriously, Rupe, is this a trick? If so just tell me?"

"Babe, have you been getting jiggy wiv the naughty salts again?"

"No, no, no, Ru, mate, I've not been getting jiggy, there's a mouse in here. It walked across my legs and ... spiked the sofa?"

"How can a mouse spike the sofa? You've totally been on the naughty salts." The man rolled his eyes again, making

Grimalkin suspect all this eye rolling was a hallmark trait of the man's. "Well, you're buying a new one. Oh, and Ams, we're out of milk. And bread. And ... basically everything. We've got no food."

"Fuck I'm starving ... " said Amelia, in an unblinking monotone. Now she was standing on a plastic chair, a rolled-up magazine outthrust in one hand, and a bag marked *Safeway* in the other, eying the deflated settee opposite as if it might spring to life.

"Seriously, Han, was this you?" said Amelia waspishly turning to Hannah, who had appeared, phantom-like, in the doorway. "Because it's not even funny."

"No," said Hannah. "I ... I was just ... doing the washing-up."

Amelia didn't answer. Her face had become beetroot-red, making her appear somewhat laughable. She let the rolled-up magazine fall from her white-knuckled grip and scuttled out the room at speed like a spider, pushing past Hannah as she went.

Grimalkin nosed cautiously from under the coffee table, feeling smug. *For three he plays!* he intoned joyously. Throughout his hauntings, he had never left any impression on the material world whatsoever. He had been able to feel, yes; and smell and taste and hear and see ... But his existence never left so much as a whisker on the fabric of the world around him. What's more, it would appear, over the ages of his hauntings, that he felt *no pain*. This made the oft-feared hazards in a cat's life – a paw on the range, or a stepped-on tail – seem to dissolve as if into thin air. The drama of the last five minutes had left him with a strange array of feelings, and questions. There was fear in the first instance, then confusion.

But there was a brand-new impulsion ... Something he had not experienced for many years ... *Mischief!*

The proverb was becoming real, just as Cat-sìth had promised. *I am invisible yet can physically affect the world ... and humans ... around me,* considered Grimalkin. He had often wondered quite *how* he would "play" during these years of the prophecy; now it was made abundantly and beautifully clear. He could pit himself against tyrants! Wage all-out wars on the mean ... He could push their wears off tables, knock their drinking vessels to the ground, claw at their legs in the night and impress his form on their skin when they least expected it. And he could do all this without so much as a twang of pain.

* * *

Grimalkin meandered into the back bedroom. He found himself drawn to this room, as the view out of this particular window never changed. In this age, above all others, he needed a reminder that he wasn't dreaming. He leaped up onto a little chest.

Ah, yes, there you are, noble steed, he intoned, tracking his eyes up the great sycamore tree, which commanded the garden as ever, its boughs now naked and etched with the frost of morning. There opposite, the same tenements soared up, reflecting the exact same echo of birdsong as they always had. Other trees were spilling their leaves, giving them a startled look, and Grimalkin felt his ear swivel forward at the *slap-slap-slap* of a pigeon's wings hitting together as it took flight from one of the narrow chimney stacks.

My, my, I used to rule this here kingdom with an iron claw! he thought nostalgically, surveying the innumerable thickets, magpie nests and garden walls that made up the expansive garden.

The room itself, however, was just as bastardised as the living room. It had been painted shocking pink and had a snooker table positioned right in the centre. A huge picture of a dandelion had been stencilled up the wall, and boxes marked Blockbuster Video lay stacked next to another television. And again there were little piles: of boxes, of empty bottles of beer and of smelly-looking clothes. Grimalkin retreated promptly.

Hannah's bedroom was, naturally, the box room – Eilidh's old store cupboard and later bedroom. To say Hannah's bed was in the room would be misleading; Hannah's bed *was* the room. The door opened to reveal a double bed and no other space above or beside it. Shelves ran the perimeter at head height from which Hannah had looped a string of little lights, and a strange rocket-shaped lamp belched green blobs in a yellowish fluid on a shelf above the headboard. A hinged table folded down over the bed so that if Hannah were to sit side-ways, she might just be able to have something resembling a table to eat and work at.

What a travesty! thought Grimalkin as he leaped up onto the bed. *This is even worse than when Eilidh inhabited this chamber. She had proper walking and storage space if nothing else. And Amelia had the cheek to suggest all the living quarters were equal in size. The bare-faced liar!*

A shelf hung skew-whiff on the wall at the foot of the bed, made from what appeared to be bamboo. On it there were a great many plastic lozenges. There was a lozenge called a "Game Boy" and another called a "Walkman". And, most curious of all, a little egg-shaped device on a chain called a "Tamagotchi". The biggest lozenge of all was a grey box with many wires coming from it called a "PlayStation".

A PlayStation, mused Grimalkin, rising up on his rear paws to sniff the strange box. *Is this a message from Cat-sìth? Must I use this to give me playing powers?* He gave the item a little prod. All of a sudden, the lid popped up on the item, giving Grimalkin such a shock he sprang back on the bed. He steadied himself, all four paws splayed as if bracing himself for another shock.

Come on, Grimalkin, be discreet. None of this numptyish behaviour. You'll give yourself away.

He felt something hard under the bedclothes. Carefully tiptoeing up to the duvet edge, he burrowed his head under it like a mole. Underneath, he found a little cylindrical tub called a "Pot Noodle". He nosed it up the bedclothes into the light, at which point he decided it must be some kind of snack, as the lettering on the side read "Great New Taste!"

Is this the age of everything-in-a-box? wondered Grimalkin. He didn't like to admit it, but he was thoroughly enjoying himself – a little room, with many curiously stacked items is a veritable heaven for any cat, though as he prodded around the various items, it often struck him that this was no fit or happy space for a human to live in. Eventually, his curiosity brought him to the dusty space behind Hannah's bedside table, where a pink folder entitled "English Literature 1A" had been shoved alongside a copy of a book called *The Prime of Miss Jean Brodie*. Grimalkin peered at the notes.

English Literature: 1A. Lecture: The fin-de-siècle and the rise of the science-fiction novel in the late nineteenth century. Lecturer: Dr Alan Pritchard.

He could tell Hannah's handwriting immediately – it was like her, nervous and small but perfectly wrought, with little loops on the "y"s and gentle upward flicks on each "k". The pages were linen-white and ordered with coloured stickers. *A conscientious scholar,* Grimalkin found himself thinking approvingly. An empty mug lay alongside, and a clutch of hairbands that sat beside several coins in a little dish marked "Bus money".

What a sorry scene, thought Grimalkin. *A bright thinker requires brighter surroundings than this!*

Moments later, Hannah emerged in the doorway, kicking the door shut behind her with her heel. Yet another lozenge was pressed against her ear into which she was talking, this one called a "Motorola".

"I have, Dad," said Hannah into the device in soft tones. "You said that last month. I *have* tried to ask them about themselves. They still don't like me."

A silence. Hannah flumped onto the bed.

"A different flat won't help. They're all too expensive anyway."

Another pause.

"I told the hardship grant people. They have me on the list, but the rent has rinsed me. Everything is so expensive here and these guys are minted. It's all just *pants*."

Grimalkin heard a wittering from the telephone lozenge getting louder.

"Oh yeah, as if that's gonna happen! Dad, it's fine, just stop it. What happened happened, okay? You couldn't help it. Uncle Pete would've wanted me to give you the money. It's nobody's fault. It just means it's quite hard to live now, that's all. But it's not that, I just hate the city. I hate the whole stupid place and its posh unpleasant people always asking me if I want to get jiggy wiv it ... Oh, it's a *phrase*, Dad, a stupid phrase ... And the greyness, and the stupid bagpipes on every corner up here. It's so ... unfriendly."

The voice on the end of the lozenge got louder as if reaching some kind of crescendo of meaning.

"Okay, okay, okay. I will. But only till then. End of October I'm coming home, and I can stay on the sofa. I'll get a job in Safeway or something. Yes, yes, *okayyy*, I'll prop my door open. No, I won't be like a little gremlin hiding in a cave. Okay, Dad, you've made your point."

Grimalkin felt the girl's loneliness deep within him. She was new to this city as he was new to this peculiar age. The age of inflatable furniture and lozenges! At least he was protected from the unkindness of humans. In Grimalkin's day, fresh-faced scholars of the university would live in these flats with host families. Their beds would be in little curtained-off corners of the kitchen. Not ideal, but at least it was near the warmth of the range. They'd get bread and dripping for breakfast included in their rental, as well as fresh linen and use of the gramophone on Sundays. There'd be a cold shower, of course, and there was no electricity for these so-called "Motorolas" or "Walkmans", but there'd be good food and comfortable chambers. There'd be respect and shared understanding. It was better than *this*.

Looking around, Grimalkin was now able to pick out the tropes of loneliness that transcend all ages. The little box of trinkets half unpacked – Eilidh had had one of these in this room. The shabby furniture in awkward positions – Eilidh had had those too. And the pictures stuck up at awkward angles, the failed attempts to create comfort, the lack of any heating or even a hook on the back of the door. And the food – the food taken into the room and eaten alone like a shamed prisoner.

"Yeah, I got an A in that," said Hannah suddenly. "The course is good. It's the only good thing." More lozenge wittering. "Dad, there's no *place* for me in halls. Geez, how many times!" The girl punched the bed in irritation. "I'm *trying* to throw myself into work, Dad! And halls wouldn't be better anyway. I went to dinner there one night – there was this huge room of people, and I could just tell by looking at them that I'd get along with none of them. None of them were my people. I need to come home and get a job and help you out. This has all just been a big mistake. Hello? Hello, Dad?"

Hannah looked at the lozenge, wiping a thumb across a little screen to clear the smudges. A yellow display presented the phrase, "Credit: £0.00. Purchase Top-Up Card".

She sighed and cast her eyes up to a high window that brought light in from the kitchen. Watching on, a sudden urge came over Grimalkin – to force himself through the fabric of time and nuzzle into this girl. *Us cats are made for moments like this,* he found himself thinking. *Yet if I nuzzled her now, she'd scream. She needs my big feline doe-eyes to gaze into hers and soothe her soul.*

Hannah rose and pulled a bag from under the bed, rustling through it. She extracted a small box in a sleeve, bearing the words "Heinz Beef Hotpot Ready Meal. Reduced! £1. **25% Extra Free!**"

Well, I never! Heinz still in existence. But for £1? A week's salary for one meal?

Staggered at the rate of inflation, Grimalkin watched on as Hannah tipped up a bag of pre-sliced bread squares till two dropped out. Mould had begun to bloom on one of them, which she scraped off with her nail. She took both the bread and the Heinz Beef Hotpot and headed out the door. Grimalkin followed, instinctively trotting by her heels through the bedroom door which appeared to pull heavily against Hannah's grasp as if desperately enacting its own emblazoned command of FIRE DOOR: KEEP SHUT. With a hopeless air, she kicked a suitcase in its path to keep it open.

The kitchen in this era was a shabby affair. It struck Grimalkin that it was probably decorated by students during a point of extreme inebriation on liquor. Parts of it, like the colour scheme, looked like pictures Grimalkin had seen on his late master's desk of Indian palaces. The walls had been painted a shocking pink, and all around, orange cupboards had been installed at human-head height, their doors wonky and misaligned. There was a gold swirly stencil daubed on the wall and a refrigerator that had been covered with pictures of various chisel-jawed men, under the phrase "The Fridge of Hotness!!!" and "Jennifer Anniston – BOOYAH!" Chipped crockery of varying designs lay piled up beside the sink, and above it all, a long tube sissled out a sickly light.

Suddenly Grimalkin's eyes widened.

MOUSE!

Quicker than a twitched ear, Grimalkin flattened to the ground and scurried over to a skirting board beside the oven, keeping his eye on the same spot the whole time.

Come, rodent, feel the clench of my JAWS!

The mouse vanished through a hole in a crumby little corner of the skirting board.

Call yourself vermin? Then come forth and face me like the scoundrel you are! I can feast in this life as much as any other – I have had a starter of Monster Munch and now I require a main course of TURGID MOUSE BELLY!

For a moment, Grimalkin crouched in front of the skirting board. It took him a while before he realised he could, of course, move *through* it. He possessed a new secret weapon in the business of rodent combat! He dissolved through the skirting board and into the cobwebby space under the oven. Hearing his claws scratch the rubber floor, the little mouse ran up and down frantically, shocked that the walls to his home had been breached.

And now I have you, cretin! thought Grimalkin with that sadistic dint that all cats – even the nicest ones – feel around cornered rodents. The poor mouse scuttled back and forth, before finding a tiny hole in the brickwork of the flat's outer wall. Flattening on its belly, it kicked its little feet frantically.

Hah! Escape? There IS NO ESCAPE for I can move through everything! thought Grimalkin. In calmer moments, he felt great shame at the visceral bloodthirsty hatred that enveloped him when in the presence of a cornered mouse. But when in the moment, there was nothing he could do to stop it. He saw red. Something primal triggered within him. The thrill of the dispatch loomed large and tantalising like a glistening guillotine about to plunge on the white neck of a French revolutionary.

Three ... two ... one ... !

Grimalkin ran headlong into the brick wall.

BUMPH!

Arrrrgh! Smolderdick and curses!

The wall had not yielded to his form. The mouse was gone. Free. It had escaped beyond the jurisdiction of the flat's realm. And Grimalkin couldn't stray ...

* * *

Grimalkin reversed back into the kitchen, his rear end held high, and his ears and whiskers drooping in the dank heaviness of disappointment. Hannah had switched on another electric tube light, which fizzled even more infuriatingly above a table by the window. Thick floral curtains hung above, crowned by a bulbous pelmet that was so shapely it made Grimalkin blush inwardly.

My, my, what revealing ... shapes! A Victorian home would never permit such curves to be on display.

Hannah leaned over to the countertop, her thin white ankles just about visible under her Winnie the Pooh gown. Astonished, Grimalkin watched as she proceeded to put the Heinz Hot Pot on a plate, stab it with a knife and then put it in a large metal box with a dial. She then turned the dial to 20 and stood waiting, as the Hot Pot pirouetted inside on a disk, like a ballerina on a lady's toilet table.

They cook their food by ... spinning it?

A savoury smell began to fill the room. Hannah stood aside the spinning plate as if waiting for an omnibus. Clearly bored, she reached into her pocket and pulled out a fistful of coins. She began counting them one by one, arranging them into little piles on the table. A few rolled off the counter onto the floor under Grimalkin's nose where they glittered beautifully in the light coming through the window.

A £1 coin!

Grimalkin spied Hannah piling several more £1 coins on the counter into little cylinders, five coins deep.

"£24.72," she muttered under her breath, dropping the coins back into her pocket. From the hallway, Grimalkin heard the instantly recognisable sound of the bathroom latch going. Glancing quickly at the dial on the cooking machine, Hannah crept out of the kitchen and into the bathroom to the soon-to-be-heard sound of a running shower.

Grimalkin batted the pound coin on the floor, sending it wobbling like a drunkard until the table leg made it fall flat, revealing Queen Elizabeth's elegant profile.

There are times when cats get ideas beyond their station of physical ability. We have all seen it: a leap grossly miscalculated; a fight picked with a cat triple the size; a sweetmeat devoured too rich and voluminous for the stomach to handle. In Victorian times, Grimalkin had been known for his remarkable bravery in the presence of Labradors in the communal garden, snarling and swiping and hissing until they scampered for shelter behind the coal shed. And so it was at this moment, on this drizzly day in 1997, that a thought crystalised in Grimalkin's mind that was perhaps a little too audacious and ambitious than he could handle ...

The Rockefeller ring.

It was a long time for Grimalkin to think back to, 1935. Despite spending so little time in each of the ages that Cat-sìth had aligned for him, Grimalkin's handle on the passage of time was blurry to say the least. What did remain crystal clear to him, however, was the flat's unique geometry: each swirl of cornice, each turn of floorboard and creak of lock. And each view – the curl of tenements as they disappeared around the crescent of the street from the bay window, or the looming sycamore from the back bedroom, above which, if you positioned yourself correctly, you could just spy the top of the flagpole at Edinburgh Castle to the north.

He also knew each squeak and fissure of the floorboards ... The same floorboards between which the Rockefeller woman had dropped her ring.

I wonder if it's still there ...

Grimalkin had, of course, seen the ring fall beneath the floorboards. But surely it had been retrieved over the intervening years? Surely a wily tradesman must've had cause to lift that floorboard to lay a pipe, or adjust a wire, and had pocketed this little treasure? Or maybe a resident (and there were many, no doubt, besides the ones Grimalkin had met) had spied a little glisten through the floor, and knelt down to inspect more closely? It would only take one curious child, one glitter under the evening lamplight ... One cold, metallic sensation against a curious finger as it panned through the subterranean dust ...

It cannot still be there. How preposterous to even think as much, Grimalkin!

Grimalkin found himself trotting into the back bedroom where the snooker table now stood. *It was over in that far corner,* thought Grimalkin, *where Mr Calvert's sink had stood in the days of Queen Victoria. And here, by the bed, was where he piled up his scholarly books from Joseph Thin's bookshop!* Hearing the noises of Hannah in the shower, Grimalkin edged over to the far corner, focusing his mind intensely on the tactile softness of the floorboards beneath his feet, feeling for any looseness or creaks that might indicate a particular board had been lifted of late.

* * *

In the quiet of the room around him, Grimalkin's ears pricked up. *Clunk.* There it was.

It was a soft noise; the sort that a human might not have even noticed under the *thud-thud-thud* of their much heavier tread. For a cat's silent paw, however, the little clunk was quite discernible. It was a quarter-sized floorboard that butted up against the vivid turquoise hearth tiles. Outside, a gossamer-like rain had started to sheet down against the sun. Those who know Edinburgh well, like Grimalkin, will know that sunshine, even at this time of year, has a remarkable habit of making an unexpected appearance. It turned out now was such a moment:

the sun had ducked out from behind a cloud and was shining perfectly on the loose floorboard. Grimalkin felt a little spur of heat as the beam crossed the tip of his paw.

Without further thought, he began drawing his paw backwards across the floorboard, claws fully extended. It took a few goes, but he achieved his aim remarkably quickly – it wasn't long before his claw nicked a corner of the loose board, pulling it up and out like a piece of jigsaw puzzle. The clatter of it landing again echoed around the room. Grimalkin flinched. Stealth was of the essence.

He peered down the gap. A dead spider. A piece of crumpled newspaper. The edge of a piece of copper piping.

Nothing.

Crouching, he lowered his head into the void, just far enough so that his whiskers pinged into the underfloor space with him. The darkness down here would have flummoxed any human, but not a cat. His eyes widened into saucers.

There!

Out of the corner of his eye, he saw a gold semicircle buried in dust.

Thank goodness I cannot feel pain for this ungainly stance would have me meowing, he thought, extending his paw nearly at right angles. He hooked the metal loop and pulled it out, before letting it plop on the floor.

Saints preserve us!

It was the ring. It was the same one alright: a soft, pink diamond, sitting chubbily in an oblong of smaller white diamonds. They were the fattest stones Grimalkin had seen on human jewellery. Usually, jewellery had gems that were vanishingly small – more like a piece of grit than a stone. This pink diamond was a veritable *pebble.*

This should fetch a handsome fistful of modern pounds, I shouldn't wonder! thought Grimalkin. With a series of repeating pats, he biffed the ring across the floor. Carefully, he patted it out into the hall, being sure to avoid the gaps between the floor-boards, and down into Hannah's bedroom, the hiss of the shower concealing the sound. There he manoeuvred it into the little nook behind the bedside table just behind the little dish marked "bus money". Hidden, but not *so* hidden that Hannah wouldn't spy it in a couple of days or feel it under her fingertips when she next picked up her copy of *The Prime of Miss Jean Brodie.*

Behold a little treat, my dear! She shall emerge, clean and squeaky from the shower to a clean and squeaky prize!

At that moment, a commotion came from the hallway. Trotting out and turning his head towards the kitchen, he spied Amelia, her horsey head bowed over a bowl and her jaws chewing. She was sneaking out the kitchen with Hannah's steaming plate of Hot Pot and bread!

That fiendish rich girl is stealing the poor girl's food! What preposterous and foul-natured villainy!

The bathroom door opened. Hannah emerged in a waft of steam, a towel around her thin form, her brown hair dangling in tendrils. She turned into the kitchen. Down the hall, Grimalkin could hear Amelia and Rupert snig-gering as the door closed to the living room behind them.

Hannah already knew what had happened before she entered the kitchen. Her face grimaced but didn't sink. She wasn't surprised. Tricks like this had been pulled on her before. Clenching and unclenching her fists, dripping with beads of water, she sank her head and moped back to her bedroom, the capacity for confrontation drained from her. A human unable to fight. Cornered.

She didn't see the ring immediately when she sat on her bed. The light coming in from the doorway was too drab to catch its great knuckles of silver and pink gemstone. It slept quite inconspicuously atop her English literature notes. There she burst into quiet little sobs, her towel still round her, and her frail, white hands lifting and falling intermit-tently to wipe tears from her eyes. She rose and kicked the suitcase away from the base of the door, letting it slam shut.

Right, this means war. Out-and-out WAR! seethed Grimalkin.

He hotfooted it towards the living room, gliding through the closed door and onto the precarious bookshelf above which Rupert and Amelia had made a little amorous nest among the blankets and deflated sofa rubber. The steaming bowl of Hot Pot straddled their laps as they gnawed and tore into the bread like wolves.

"You will go out later, Rupe?" said Amelia under concealed giggles. "I feel . . . like . . . really mean now."

"Serves her right for being such a boring munter," said Rupert in a long, drawn-out tone. "It might be the thing that finally makes her come out with us and get jiggy and fucking grow a personality so she isn't the human form of fucking beige. Also, she *is* getting out that box room. Daddy says I could double the rent. It'll teach her a lesson to not be such a tight-arsed cheapskate."

I'll teach YOU a lesson, you oafish CAD, thought Grimalkin, taking to his heels and clawing up the side of the bookshelf before launching himself, belly-first, into the epicentre of the steaming dish.

Edinburgh Evening News

Monday 1 December 1997

Girl Finds Million Dollar Ring in Digs.

A former University of Edinburgh student was stunned to find an 82-carat ring in her rented room in Marchmont.

The ring is due to go under the hammer at Sotheby's this afternoon and has already secured an £800,000 reserve based on rumours the precious stone once belonged to a member of the Rockefeller family.

In an exclusive interview, the ring's finder, Hannah Tinsley, originally from Exeter, Devon, commented:

"I'm still in shock. I had heard the flat was once occupied by famous folk, but I never thought I'd find something like this. It's the stuff of dreams."

For Miss Tinsley, the discovery of the coveted gem could not have come at a better time:

"My dad has been in financial dire straits and I had to drop out of uni. Now I can pursue my dream English degree nearer to home where I can support my dad to get back up on his feet. I still feel like I'm dreaming!"

Edinburgh Evening News tried to reach out to the flat's owner via agency Grant Letting Associates, but no one was available to comment.

Grimalkin's Observations

Decoration:	Pastel colours. Everywhere.
Humans:	Amelia, that unpleasant horse-girl; Rupert, her tousle-haired accomplice; Hannah, the English literature genius and soon-to-be millionaire.
Technology:	Lozenge cord-free telephone.
Monarch:	Queen Elizabeth II.

Seventh Haunting, September 2008

S OMETIMES A CAT SENSES A malevolent presence even before it opens its eyes.

His eyes tightly shut, Grimalkin became aware of a redness behind his eyelids. He was either outside or staring into a light. Then his nose pinched, and whiskers trembled: there was an odd scent in the air. There came moments later a heady inrush of a most foul smell: sour alcohol. And then another: sweat. And then another: the stench of bad breath.

He opened his eyes.

It took a moment for him to locate himself. Across his eyeline, a blackberry vine rose and fell gently in mid-air, the sky beyond it deep and unfathomably blue. To his left, the handsome side of an Edinburgh tenement shimmered into focus. He could now feel the dry bristle of sun-warmed grass underneath him. He stretched out his paws, lifting his head momentarily to take in the innumerable glittering windows of the rear-facing side of Marchmont Crescent. A singing voice came trickling out of an upper flat where net curtains billowed gently in the breeze. Grimalkin's ear swivelled in its direction. This music was strange, involving a cacophony of drums and various instruments. All around, the once-black stonework looked cleaner: here and there, entire slabs had been replaced with brand-new sandstone blocks, making the tenement look like a patchwork quilt rather than the frightfully huge soot-blackened edifice of yore. Facing into the sun, the tenement's great side took on a reddish hue in the evening light, and Grimalkin's eye became quickly preoccupied by a couple of amorous pigeons who strutted up and down the gutterwork, their feathers tinged crimson and their affections signalling the beginning of the late summer mating season.

Ah, the furrows and grasses of my old back garden, thought Grimalkin. *What a wondrous scene on an evening such as this, were it not bastardised by this foul bouquet of odours.*

Looking around, he found he was still within the territory of flat 7/7 – the large wrought-iron railings carving up the tenement gardens into their various portions clearly placed him within its jurisdiction. It was famed on the street for being the segment in which the handsome sycamore tree was planted, whose upper branches gave Grimalkin many an entertaining bird watch in the 1890s.

A catarrh-y cough sent Grimalkin's pelt ruching along his back. Just to the left was a human seated in a garden chair. He was a largish man, around sixty in human years, but with sharp beady eyes. Unnerved, Grimalkin traced his outline slowly from the top of his head, down along his oversized chin to his hands, which were dainty and pearlescent like marble. Little black dots covered his cheeks where a beard would have formed had he not shaved, and his shirt and trousers were dark, but not *so* dark that they didn't show up an unpleasant mix of stains from the careless consumption of oily foods. One hand was in a large packet of crisps that were caked in orange dust (which clearly accounted for the orange trouser stains) while his other was clenched around a plastic device that was guiding an arrow across a television screen that bore the phrase "www.londonstockexchange.com".

Hmmm, what terrible little eyes, thought Grimalkin, remembering how the most vicious of dogs tended to be the ones with pinched-together features.

"Arrrgh-upmh!"

Grimalkin juddered. A few paces off, a slobbering pitbull dog was lounging on the grass, its lead attached to a stake that had been driven into the ground.

Fie, beast, you diabolical spawn of Lucifer! seethed Grimalkin, his tail fur bristling up.

"Urrrr-uph, uph, uph!" said the dog.

Approach me and your gizzard will be torn asunder, you miserable, snub-nosed, drooling numpty!

Grimalkin stalked over to the dog, who of course remained oblivious to his physical presence. As he neared, however, Grimalkin noted the dog's breathing had become broken, its ears swivelling and its eyes fixing on the grass where Grimalkin's paws were making gentle imprints on the lawn.

"Grrr ... AR-RAH-RAH-RAH!" growled the dog, launching itself at the grass and pulling out to the extent of its tethered lead.

"Shut up, Spike," said the fat man at his table.

Grimalkin froze. He was suddenly struck with an intense feeling of déjà vu. The dog pacified and slumped its belly down onto the grass. Memories of an earlier age started to flicker out of nowhere in Grimalkin's brain, like dust under the beam of a torch. He scanned the man's hulking body once again ... The grizzly bear eyes; the rounded, gargoyle-like shoulders that thrust forward like a vulture's wings. He now noticed how peculiar his hands were – pallid and white, with filthy undersides and fingernails. And that smell on the air: stale alcohol.

Hang about, I recognise this man! And I recall the awful character that attends him! HE was the one attempting to seduce Elaine in 1969! Was his name ... Keith?

Grimalkin leaped up onto the table that the man was working at, feeling his already acute dislike of him growing stronger. It clearly *was* Keith – the same oily man who had met the party of moon revellers at Edinburgh Waverley station and who he had spied trying to slide his hand down Elaine's back on Calton Hill. He had evidently come into some money in recent years, as the shabby leather jacket had been replaced with a tailored suit and an expensive-looking watch. His hair had turned grey and receded so far up his temples that it appeared to make an arrow that pointed down his scalp. Along with his gut, which now protruded over his belt, the only other difference to the Keith of 1969 was his dentistry: instead of a row of tobacco-stained tombstones, his teeth now resembled a line of perfect white dominoes and had clearly been replaced with artificial counterparts. They dazzled distressingly in the sun and made Grimalkin feel nauseous. Mixed with the odour of sweat and alcohol came the cheesy smell of the orange things Keith was gnawing at – like the Monster Munches of the nineties but more worm-like.

Grimalkin inched stealthily across the table, being careful to remain mouse-quiet as the dog still sat nearby. There was Keith's wallet and scattered change (the pounds still bearing Queen Elizabeth's face), a box of cigarettes, and a set of keys all gathered around a fob bearing the words "Aston Martin". The table itself was peppered with bird droppings but Keith didn't seem to mind, even letting some of his crisps fall onto the splatters before picking them back up and dropping them into his podgy little mouth.

He must live in the flat if Cat-sìth has placed me in his company, thought Grimalkin. *Oh, that I didn't have to play! Oh, that I could venture up those stairs and say "wazzup" to the old place . . . if indeed that is the salutation of this infernal age!*

Several gadgets were positioned alongside the screen Keith was peering into, with various labels – "USB mouse splitter", "Bluetooth dongle" and "ZIP drive". The half-sense-half-nonsense of these phrases made Grimalkin wonder if they were part of some kind of human in-joke in this new age. "Anyone require a mouse-splitter?" "Yes, it's in the ZIP drive beside the bureau." *Anyhow, was Bluetooth not a renowned human leader of the tenth century or thereabouts?* All the while, Grimalkin could not take his eyes off Keith's filthy talon-like fingernails and couldn't help but wonder if he had cleaned under them in the intervening years between 1969 and today.

With a side glance to the dog, who had fallen into a slobbery sleep on the grass, Grimalkin stealthily tiptoed into the centre of Keith's desk and parked himself between the man's bad-tempered face and the screen. Part of Grimalkin wanted to immediately cause Keith mischief for his foul behaviour in 1969, but a slightly bigger compulsion to see what he was doing won out. At least for now. With the stealthy grace of a cougar, Grimalkin tiptoed across all of Keith's technological devices, knowing one misplaced paw could trigger this man's suspicions. On the screen, lines snaked up and down above numbers which seemed to change multiple times a second. Beside them, names of various companies were listed, some of which Grimalkin recognised from former eras, like "Lloyds Banking Group" and "Sainsbury's" and others which seemed entirely new like "Vodafone" and "Lehman Brothers".

Grimalkin gazed back at Keith's beady eyes, which were inches away from his. Deep within their dark orbs, Grimalkin could detect a restless and almost terrifying hunger. A hunger for money.

"Selling, why are they selling so ruddy quick, what have they ruddy-well seen?" snorted Keith through a mouthful of orange dust.

He swore loudly and broke away, foiling the beautiful autumn late afternoon that was starting to draw out the colours of the garden. Leaning down to the grass, he returned with a blue and orange tin marked IRN-BRU.[1] Grimalkin blinked as a fine mist doused his whiskers at the same moment Keith plucked the ring pull back before tipping his head and glugging down its fluid like a sentient steam iron. This fluid, too, was orange and made Grimalkin begin to wonder whether all foodstuffs in this day and age were orange-coloured and orange-flavoured.

Does this so-called "IRN-BRU" taste like cheese as well? It doesn't smell like cheese.

Grimalkin couldn't help himself. He simply had to sample the decade's cuisine, and the numbers on the screen hadn't been especially interesting to him. Ensuring the dog was still in the midst of a deep slumber, and just as Keith placed the can back on the table beside him, Grimalkin took one swipe of the paw and biffed the can to its side.

---

[1] The popularity of IRN-BRU in Scotland often gives rise to the apocryphal affirmation that Scotland is the only country in the world not to have Coca-Cola as its most popular soft drink.

"Oh, effing drat it." Keith lurched back as orange fizz trickled through the slats of the garden table onto his lap. But just as Grimalkin was about to sample the juice, he felt Keith's icy, paper hand pass through his ghostly feline form to the right of the tin. Grimalkin had felt other lives pass through his form before ... Normally this event gave rise to no feelings whatsoever. Occasionally, such as with Eilidh, a hand or a leg passing through his body gave a little frisson of heat like a warm draught coming under a door on a cold day. But this man's human presence gave rise to a feeling so icy and damp that Grimalkin leaped off the table and into a nearby hydrangea bush without so much as a second thought. There he tried to lick his fur, which still reeled with pain like a chilblained toe.

I am tired of all this, thought Grimalkin. *Ruddy tired. All this haunting business ... all this thwarted curiosity. Get me calm.*

The voice from earlier trickled down from the high window again.

Have mercy on me, Cat-sìth! Get me sleep! I'm having another of my bicentennial supernatural crises. I feel profoundly UN-groovy!

Grimalkin had got used to these crises. Sometimes, during his hauntings, he found himself feeling not only ambivalent towards the complete and total oblivion of death, but actively craving it. To sleep and to *never* dream ... surely that is any cat's most sought-after prerogative anyhow? He skulked moodily in amongst the shrubbery that ran the length of the garden, watching the bugs crawl over the newly spilled leaves, and hearing the faint laughter of students trickle down from nearby windows. There was that autumnal nip in the air, and the hoppy scent of the Edinburgh breweries smelled especially atmospheric and pungent. *How alive everything is,* he thought as a robin landed on an old pile of roof slates that lay stacked in a corner beside a shed. *How veritably alive. Every tiny heart beating. Every animal's head set on thoughts of survival for the coming winter. My, I really feel rum again. Not in the mood for mischief at all. I feel less like a gambolling kitten than ever I did.*

He thought of the Rockefeller lady, and JM Barrie, and the 1960s moon watchers – the moustachioed man in the driving seat of the small car and short-skirted Elaine who was fondled by this same man sitting here in the garden. Had he experienced comeuppance? Had he lived his whole life treating people this way, tricking others out of money? It struck Grimalkin that most humans do their best, and relatively few are truly bad ... Most of them are alone and scared. He knew this because he had seen them in their most private of moments. And by Jove, were they *different* in their private moments.

Where were all those others now? The kindly, teddy bear-chinned man who tended to Eilidh? John's mother with the big hair in the kitchen? The student Hannah and her scared eyes? Married? Children? Happy? Miserable?

Grimalkin cast his eyes up to the second-floor windows of the tenement. His eyes widened as one of the dirt-sucking machines droned out its satanic din. Someone had evidently dropped a crumby biscuit.

He slid his gaze to directly above where he was. There it was. The noble old flat. With its stag window above the door, and box room and fairy cake cornices in the lounge. Did *it* feel any different? Of course not. It was bricks and mortar; it was merely imbued with the life of others. It was both Grimalkin's liberty and his prison; the epicentre to his thoughts which kernelled and twisted over the course of his time-warping sojourn in the twentieth century. A frantic century. A fascinating and tragic century whose big crises were mirrored in the anguish and joy of everyday Scottish people in this great city.

That flat and its inhabitants are all I know, thought Grimalkin, thinking of the myriad other cats in the world who only ever knew one set of rooms, one space, one view.

A yelp came from over the stone wall at the foot of the garden. Children. Grimalkin eyed two boys as they leaped over the wall easy as fleas and hid behind a shed. Soon after, two girls appeared in school uniform, clambering over the wall in pursuit. One of the boys balanced on an upturned metal tin bath, half concealed in the leaf-strewn autumn grass. "Ner-ner-n-n-er-ner. This is OUR shed, finders keepers, losers weepers. Access denied."

Ner-ner-n-n-er-ner-YOURSELVES, thought Grimalkin, reeling from the shrieks of children, which seemed largely unchanged across the centuries. *Hang about, I recognise that bath ... That's Eilidh's tin bath! Why, I was bathed in that the day I came home as a kitten in 1887!*

It was indeed the same bath, with the same branding on its side and the same scorched dimple in its upturned backrest which Eilidh had caused by letting the fireside poker rest against it unawares. The same one that had hung on the wall of the box room all those years ago. Grimalkin sniffed it. The same metallic scent! Exactly as Grimalkin recalled it on Victorian evenings when Eilidh would fill it for the master's Sunday ablutions.

And what was this ... ? An oblong item lying alongside, half-rotted! Grimalkin prodded it with his paw, turning it over. A goo of muddy rot and insect larvae flipped into view. Half the thing had rotted away, but Grimalkin could just about recognise the thick boar bristles, and the brass plate now discoloured and blooming red with rust ... The nameplate bearing Eilidh's surname – *MacNeil*. The back-scritcher!

Why, if it isn't Eilidh's work tools, left forlorn to fall to ruination! The cheek!

A cry came up. Keith at his outdoor workstation had heard the children scampering into his garden quarter.

"Oi, oi, you ugly little buggers, clear off," he cried out in his thick Yorkshire accent, which had become nasal with age. The boys ducked behind the shed sniggering. "Oi, I can see you!" Keith responded more intently, craning his neck towards the crevice behind the shed, where the children squatted, giggling

199

and shushing each other. He lumbered up to a stand and waddled over to his dog, who had stirred with the commotion. "Bugger off, you nasty little runts, or I'll set my dog on you."

As Keith approached, the children behind the shed began to chuckle again. In a giggling scurry, they darted out from behind the shed and over the wall just escaping Keith's view.

"Don't you laugh at me, you wretched toerags," said Keith, suddenly becoming frightening, a vein pulsating on his temple. In a rage, he picked up Eilidh's brush and lobbed it after one of the boys, who narrowly avoided its trajectory before disappearing into the communal door of one of the tenements opposite. "Ratbags," said Keith under his breath. "Christ. Some of us have money to make."

Grimalkin felt a bubble of rage rise in him. Hardly stopping to think, he turned and galloped back over the garden table that served as Keith's desk, beating him back. He leaped up and looked at the screen. The figures of Keith's share portfolio climbed up and sank on the screen in lines like writhing worms. Grimalkin eyed the keyboard. One button loomed large: DELETE. He jabbed it with his paw, again and again and again. The computer started to make noises that even Grimalkin, as a non-tech savvy cat, could appreciate were bad noises. One by one the little writhing lines on the screen began to vanish as messages popped up asking "CAUTION! Highly volatile share! Are you sure you wish to sell?" which Grimalkin correctly assumed was best responded to with another jab of the DELETE button.

Keith's ears pricked up to the dissatisfied chimes of his screen, his pace over the grass quickening and his little dark bear eyes fixed unblinkingly ahead. "What? Christ, what on earth?" A sour, bilious anger seized his face, making each of his veins rise to the surface like spaghetti. "What? WHAT? *NO! NO! NO!*" The dog started barking and tugging at its stake, sensing the brightness of his master's panic.

Calmly, with a twist of his tail tip, Grimalkin minced over the desk and upturned the tin of IRN-BRU all over the computer keyboard with one smooth bat of his paw. Then, with a satisfied prance, he sashayed down off the table, landing on the grass beside the table leg, whereupon he tilted his head and lapped up the little trickle of orange fizz that fell from the table. It ran down the back of his mouth and fizzled along his tongue, before falling into his belly where it tickled like bird feathers.

Oh no. Oh dear, no. Not for me. Oh my, that really does taste rather vile.

Shortly after the events described above, on 15 September 2008, the 2008 Global Economic Crisis commenced. Despite popular opinion continuing to link the crash's tipping point to the collapse of American investment firm Lehman Brothers, a growing body of economic scholarship attributes the collapse to a more mercurial set of economic factors.

Grimalkin's Observations

Decoration:	Unknown but brickwork cleaner.
Humans:	Nasty Man from 1969 reappears. Time has not been kind to his gut and general demeanour.
Technology:	Many whirring devices.
Monarch:	Queen Elizabeth II.

Eighth Haunting,
September 2022

"**L**OOK AT THIS PHILISTINISM, VIEWERS! Not only have they left drips aplenty but they've painted over this lovely beehive handle!"

Oh, merciful Lord, give me strength, seethed Grimalkin. *What foolery must I endure in this age?*

"Time to get it cleaned up with Brasso, the sweet nectar of the metal gods!"

My, this human is a knavish numpty, whoever he is.

Achy and with a heavy mind, Grimalkin arched his back reluctantly into the air. The familiar dimensions of Marchmont Crescent's living room greeted him. Here and there, various naked bulbs glowed, and the room had that makeshift feel of a place recently having assumed new occupancy. Precarious piles of plastic boxes dotted the room, and plastic bags from establishments unknown to Grimalkin such as "Lidl" and "TK Maxx". Dustsheets lay draped over the fireplace and pinned across the Edinburgh presses, and little screwdrivers congregated in corners by the electric plug sockets, their coloured knobbly ends like lollipops. Outside, the rain lashed down in great splinters, giving the room a warm and cosy feel despite its bareness. It was a room full of intrigue – the sort of boxy, creviced room that immediately piques the curiosity of any cat. Only the inane spiel of chatter marred the otherwise agreeable atmosphere.

From whence does this confounded dandyish voice emerge?

Grimalkin peered round to find the voice was coming from above him: near the doorway to the room, a man teetered atop an A-frame ladder, like an acrobat about to leap, while chirruping and gesticulating inanely into a little screen which he held out in front of himself.

What sweet hell?

There was something about the man's quick movements, dark floppy hair and oddly contorted frame that Grimalkin found both annoying and beguiling in equal measure. His childish enthusiasm suggested he must have been not long from the family nest – a milksop of sorts – though the fullness of his face and presence of a somewhat flabby belly made Grimalkin think he was perhaps older than his body language suggested.[1]

---

[1] The editor takes issue with this. The man sounds, if anything, like he was slightly wide-boned.

The man climbed down the ladder like a monkey and clipped the little screen into a snake-like bracket attached to the door frame. "Golly, I need to get a life," he said suddenly, in halftones, in the way an actor might when exiting the stage after an exhausting scene.

He disappeared to the left, into what Grimalkin knew was Eilidh's old box room. Grimalkin trotted after him but no sooner had he poked his head around the threshold than he reared up on his paws, as the man was returning with something clanky and metallic in his hand. Shortly after, he procured a little grey bucket containing a tin of Brasso and various scrubbing brushes.

Oh, Brasso! That takes me back. Maybe he is about to restore the brasses to their former lustre? thought Grimalkin, trotting over with renewed energy. *Oh, mighty good for him. Get them shining like Eilidh did, good sir!*

Something about the man's foppish energy and drive had an oddly contagious effect on Grimalkin. This was no doubt augmented by the heady smell of Brasso (which took his mind straight back to Eilidh's buffing rag). *That smell!* Suddenly, he felt the frustrations of the former decades – the cruelties he had witnessed and the meanness of spirit – begin to ebb away. In their place came an upswell of kittenish mischief. Even a cat of extensive wisdom and knowledge still remembers the fresh, raw adrenalin-joy of the hunts of their youth . . .

High on the fumes, Grimalkin began scampering up and down the room.

My, what fun. Zoooooooooorrrooooooom.

The proportions of the familiar spaces he knew so well blurred in and out of view.

Yahhooooooo. Hello, sir, how's tricks? Broooommmzzzzoooooom!

Despite his speed, he was still able to note a fair few changes in the flat; enough, at least, to realise the entire place had been covered in a sort of lumpy and bubbly magnolia wallpaper that resembled gravel. As he skurried past the front door, he spied that the stained-glass window, depicting the stag, had been beautifully cleaned. All the fireplaces had also been brought back, their cardboard coverings torn off and propped up alongside. Here and there large posters lined the wall, ungainly and huge as if they had originally been meant to be displayed in much larger surroundings. One poster that had been pinned up in the front bedroom bore the words *Les Misérables*, while another one, still curled at the edges from living in its little tube, bore the words *Phantom of the Opera*.

Kitchen utensils in plastic boxes lay strewn throughout the hallway, alongside piles of stuffy-looking books, and innumerable letters on the doormat addressed to "THE NEW OCCUPIER".

"Alex ... Alex ... *Lynxyyyy!*"

Grimalkin's right ear rotated in the direction of the voice. *There is a second human at large!* He trotted towards the kitchen only to feel a warm shiver along his flank as he walked straight through the path of a girl. She was petite with a fringe, and from the softness of her call and the easy clothes she was wearing, Grimalkin could tell immediately she was the Brass Man's partner.

Grimalkin tailgated the girl as she approached the man in the doorway, who had placed some little white buds in his ears. "Lynxy!" The girl tapped him gently on the shoulder.

"Achh, bloody hell, stop doing that creeping up thing, Otter!" said the Brass Man. "Gee willikins, it makes me jump out of my skin."

"I called you like six times," responded the girl with a frustrated sweep of her hand through the air and a roll of her eyes. There was a firmness to the girl's voice that made Grimalkin believe her to be a fearless interlocutor with the Brass Man's chaotic energy despite her small stature. "You did say you'd make dinner, Lynx, and the baba's hungry in my tum. He wants his grub-grub."

"Oh, the bubba in your tum should learn to be … *be patient*," said the Brass Man with a flounce, screwing the lid on the Brasso tin, and stepping down the ladder. "Sorry, Otter, time ran away with me. Is just, like, a ready meal okay? Or a Kiev? Or how about a sinful?"

"We've had a takeaway twice already this week, Lynx."

"Yeah, okay, okay. You're right. I'll go to the shops now."

"And … Lynx … " said the girl. Grimalkin could tell she was limbering up for a more delicate conversation; one which could escalate if she didn't approach it with tact.

"Yes, Otter … "

"I know the TikTok and the brass is fun and stuff, but do you think we should probably unpack our moving boxes first? We don't even have a bedroom yet or somewhere to sit in the evenings. I don't want to have the shiniest doorknobs but a pile of Ryman's stack boxes for a dining table."

"Yes, of course, Otter."

At standing, Grimalkin was remarked by how tall the man was. He loomed over the girl, who vanished into his big arms as they hugged.

"Sorry, Lynx, I don't want to be a killjoy."

"No, it's okay, Otter, you're right. I need to be told sometimes. I'll get the room in order and I'll take some time off in lieu from work on Thursday, and maybe we can go to that antiques place and see if we can get a table for the kitchen and a sofa bed for the spare room?"

"Sounds good, Lynx."

"Oh, and um ..." said the man, pushing his glasses up his nose and grabbing a set of keys from a little dish on a makeshift hall table, "how about that nice pork racky thing for dins? The Sainsbury's Local pork racky thing? With chippies?"

"Sounds lovely, Lynx!" said the girl, giving the man another hug.

A silence fell ... A loaded silence which Grimalkin assumed must be communicative on a non-verbal level, since the pair seemed to know and love each other very much.

The front door slammed; a familiar *ker-chunk* followed by three tinkling high notes as the key escutcheon knocked against the keyhole. It was a pleasant sound – familiar and comforting – that remained unchanged down the ages. To Grimalkin, it sounded as warm and comforting as if Eilidh had herself extended her warm hand through time to tickle him behind the ear.

In the newfound silence, the girl went over to a little squat hall table and pulled open a drawer. From there, she took out a little oblong box before padding down the hall and turning into the back bedroom. Grimalkin trotted after her.

My, the old chamber looks fair dandy, mused Grimalkin, entering the back bedroom. The walls had been stripped of the bubbly magnolia wallpaper and had been painted a lovely vibrant teal. A mahogany wardrobe stood in one corner, and the fireplace fizzed and crackled with little orange flames, looking exactly as it did the day he curled up, sighing his last sentient breaths that day in 1902. A gorgeous pine smell filled the room, along with the starchy smell of newly ironed clothes as the girl had an ironing board out and was halfway through laundering. Grimalkin leaped up onto the bed and then the ironing board being sure to be as light on the paw as possible. He was on a poltergeist life, and he didn't want to cause undue alarm to this nice girl who had temporarily turned to search for something in the wardrobe.

The clothes were some kind of uniform, as several identical blue smocks and trousers lay piled up, each smock bearing the emblem NHS LOTHIAN.

Trousers? A smock on a lady? Rather unfit for the workplace, is it not? thought Grimalkin, in spite of himself. Often he felt his views had been made thoroughly contemporary over the course of his hauntings and had shaken off all their former Victorian prejudices and views. Other times, he couldn't have felt more Victorian than if he had been traversing the Forth Rail Bridge on a steam train while sitting atop Charles Dickens' lap.

The girl perched on the edge of the bed, the box from the drawer in the hallway clutched in her hand. Grimalkin could now just about spy the writing on the box: COVID ANTIGEN LATERAL FLOW TEST. Bemused, Grimalkin watched as the girl extracted several curious pieces of plastic, one of which – a sort of plastic stalk – she proceeded to shove up her nose. This prompted her to do a big sneeze, which made Grimalkin leap in the air and dart under the ironing board with a racing heart.

What incarnate torture is this lady inflicting on herself? wondered Grimalkin in a sort of frightened bafflement. His eyes followed on in heightening trepidation as the girl located the plastic stalk in her *other* nostril, before sneezing prodigiously once again.

What in the tarnation?

The girl then dipped the plastic bud into a little vial of fluid before fastidiously dripping some of the fluid onto a plastic tab.

My, the woman is a clandestine apothecarist! She is using her husband's absence to brew lethal tinctures from sneezes and vials! Why, she must be brought to book!

210

But something didn't sit right with Grimalkin about that conjecture. The girl didn't *seem* like the sort who would run a covert drug laboratory while her husband disappeared momentarily to purchase the evening meal. She had neither the character nor the craggy-faced appearance of a secret drug baron. After several moments examining her telephone, the girl turned with a sigh and inspected one of the bits of plastic.

"Negative," she said in a chipper voice. "No day off for me tomorrow, Tabitha!"

* * *

A little cat had just walked into the room. As the years had gone on, Grimalkin had become a little less hostile at seeing other cats, knowing of course that he had no hope of sparring with them in his supernatural form. He was also beginning to feel a kinship with his fellow cats, whose short lease on planet Earth, when viewed from his ethereal plane, seemed puny and somehow pitiable. Grimalkin found himself feeling a particular affinity for this cat, who was a grey tortoiseshell but also sported a marmalade-coloured flank as he did, and who also had the same intelligent sparkle about the eyes. The cat sniffed the air and seemed attuned to the fact that there was something different about the room. Grimalkin could tell, in that ineffable way all cats can, that she was female and was spoilt rotten by her humans. He also could tell, in an even more ineffable way, that this cat shared the same blood as he did and was, quite possibly, a great, great, great descendent of his once-insatiable loins.

Suddenly, the cat meowed in Grimalkin's direction.

Well, blast and bah humbug to you too, madam! thought Grimalkin, rising his back into an arch.

"What's the matter, Tabbikins?" said the girl, who was clearly bemused at the cat's sudden querulous attitude. Grimalkin approached and circled around the cat, his back still arched. But the cat's eyes darted around unfocused, clearly unable to perceive Grimalkin's ghostly form despite sensing his delicate, near-inaudible contact on the floorboards in front of her.

Feeling a little rush of sympathy at her helplessness, Grimalkin's stance settled, and he inched closer to the little cat and nuzzled into its neck in an attempt at reconciliation. Alarmed at the invisible contact on her fur, the cat charged out of the room in so frenzied a manner that her legs positively ran mid-air for a moment, before they developed traction with the floorboards.

"Tabitha Pushkin Howard, calm yourself!" said the girl after the little feline, who galloped down the hallway straight into the path of the Brass Man returning through the door with the groceries.

"Have you just done a poo, puss?" said the man.

"No, Lynx, she's just behaving really weird. Have you been cat-nipping her?"

"No? We haven't even got her toys out yet, they're still all packed away."

"Silly puss!" responded the girl. "I don't know what's up with her. It's like she's always got the zoomies but she hasn't even done a poo today."

"Silly puss," echoed the man, attempting to grab the cat as she darted past him up the hallway.

"I'm just going to do that last tiny bit of painting before the brush dries out, that okay?" said the Brass Man, entering the kitchen with the ladder under one arm. In the corner was an open pot of paint where the Brass Man had been painting the wall. With a sigh, he placed the bag of groceries on the countertop and climbed the ladder, a paintbrush in one hand and a little pot of paint cupped in the palm of the other.

Well, if my great-grandchild isn't going to give me the time of day, I might as well try and commune with the man.

Intrigued to see what the man was painting, Grimalkin placed his two forepaws on the side of the ladder, leaning his weight into its side and craning his neck at the ceiling.

"Bloody hell, what the?!"

With a little *clunk,* the ladder gave way, shifting slightly to the right, clearly giving the Brass Man a significant shock. He responded, rather comically, by flailing his ungainly limbs skyward and sending a tongue of yellow paint streaking across the kitchen's white countertop.

"Lynxy? Are you okay?"

"Oh, b****. What the f***ing f****ity f**k. Did you touch the ladder?"

213

"What? The ladder? I'm still in here," returned the girl's voice from the back bedroom.

"What? I'm so confused. The bloody ladder moved! Like, of its own accord! Where are you?"

"The *bedroom*, Lynx!"

"Are you sure?"

"Yes!"

The man frowned, his mop of hair ruched up into a mini set of spikes which seemed comically expressive of the shock he had just endured.

"Seriously, Lynx, you need to be more careful. Don't do things so quickly," said the girl.

"No, seriously," protested the man. "Something moved the ladder. I swear it. Something jostled it to the side. This flat is weird, I'm telling you ... "

"Strange. And weird how Tabitha's been this afternoon as well."

The man stepped cautiously down the ladder, dabbing a bead of yellow paint off his cheek, which had turned white with shock. He proceeded to get a cloth and wipe down the countertop glumly like a recently rebuked schoolboy. "Don't worry, Lynx," said the girl supportively. "These things happen. At least we didn't get it on the IKEA rug."

"I think this place is haunted," said the man. "And I reckon Tabitha thinks so too."

* * *

There comes a time in a cat's playful existence when a huge, soporific calm falls over them. The havoc-wreaking work is completed; the vase is smashed, the curtains shredded and the tablecloth torn asunder. They have slain the mouse, maimed the bird and squarely punctured the lung of the rat. It behoves all cats at this time to thoroughly contemplate their mastery: to assess the fractured shards on the floor with a sniff or two or settle down to devour their catch before taking a well-earned snooze. It is perhaps, at this time, that all thinking cats are at their most philosophical, and it definitely felt that way to Grimalkin as he observed the young couple, some hours later, sitting on the stacked boxes in the living room with their dinner on their laps as they spoke of recent events.

I think I have the measure of this pair, Grimalkin thought, gazing at the couple through half-closed eyes. He was sitting on a pile of cushions that were shrunk and contorted in a vacuum-sealed bag. In the intervening hours, the Brass Man had begun painting the lounge a beautiful deep blue, and on the mantlepiece, the girl had positioned two brass railway lanterns that glistened under the flicker of a nearby candle. A fine-looking model train was displayed in the Edinburgh press, and on a bureau alongside stood several pictures – a wedding photo, a picture of Tabitha and a little montage of what looked like otters. A house was becoming a home.

The girl had also hung pictures from the wall, at carefully thought-out intervals, and rather than being held in place by a nail, were instead hanging on little pieces of wire from the picture rail. Grimalkin had not seen pictures hanging from the picture rail since the Edwardian times, and there was something pleasant about watching them sway slightly as they caught the breeze of someone passing by them. It reminded him of how the carthorses outside would send Mr Calvert's great oil paintings swinging gently in the 1800s.

Blimey, the 1800s, thought Grimalkin. It gave him a vertiginous feeling when he thought of how much time he had existed across, as if he was staring over the lip of a bridge down onto a monstrous set of rapids churning and frothing. *One hundred and twenty years! I ought to write a book one day.*

Beyond the window, the streetlight clicked on, illuminating a little mist of drizzle around its yellow globe.

To think they've felt me but not seen me, mused Grimalkin wistfully, looking at the pair opposite, who were observing the television in a half-cuddle. *If only I could tell them what I've seen in this room, across the years. They seem the sort who would be interested. Particularly Brass Man with his love of old things. Brass Man and I would probably get on. Or hate each other. It is difficult to tell, alas.*

The cat Tabitha walked in and proceeded to bury herself in a box of clothes, much to the mirth of the couple, her long, lithe body twisting and contorting in ecstasy.

And as for you, thought Grimalkin, gazing at the little cat while being sure to remain perfectly still. *How many lives have you expended, I wonder? You have eaten through at least two, I dare say, with your reckless skittering alone!*

A small gasp came from the sofa. Grimalkin looked over to see that the girl had placed her hand over her mouth. Something was being said on the television that was causing shock, as shortly after, the Brass Man joined the girl in wearing the same incredulous expression. Both became still and fixated on the screen.

Grimalkin twisted an ear.

"A few moments ago, Buckingham Palace announced the death of Her Majesty Queen Elizabeth II."

A weird silence filled the room. In the quiet, an image crept into Grimalkin's brain before flickering away like a reflection from glass: it was of the beaming face of Mr McTulloch wrapped in Union Jack bunting – the emcee at the street party at the time of Queen Elizabeth II's coronation in 1953.

"The Palace has just issued this statement: 'The Queen died peacefully this afternoon at Balmoral. The King and Queen Consort will remain at Balmoral this evening and will return to London tomorrow.'"

The couple gawped, appearing almost frozen with shock. The little cat jumped up onto the man's lap and sniffed the girl's arm, meowing at their sudden stillness.

"Genuinely," said the girl, "I can't believe it. It was like she'd never die. I thought she'd go on forever ... "

Grimalkin tiptoed over to underneath the television. A newsreader spoke while the picture on the screen seemed to be a static image of a set of palace gates.

"Crazy," said the Brass Man, running his hand through his untidy hair and shifting a leg up underneath him. "It's weird to think people would've been in this living room when she was coronated. If only we could see through time."

Ha! Very good. And most amusing, thought Grimalkin. *Well, I can see through time, sir, and I counsel you to not quip and absorb yourself in idle talk upon hearing of Her Majesty's passing. May she rest in peace and long live the ... I say, who would it be now?*

"So Charlie-boy is king?" said the girl, as if overhearing Grimalkin's thoughts.

"Yup. King Charles III," said the Brass Man. "Sounds kind of weird, doesn't it."

Outside, the sky was turning an inky grey. Rain battered on the glass, drawing in the wheaty scent of the McEwans brewery through the half-opened window; a constant over time that seemed to gather up all of Grimalkin's memories of the city in its fragrant tang and hold them together like flecks of gold in a panner's sieve. Back in Victorian times, it'd be braided in with a myriad other smells, pleasant and foul: manure, tar ... The ammonia of the saddlery on Thirlestane Road ... And of course, coal smoke. Coal smoke viscous and thick as ectoplasm.

Grimalkin felt empty; a curious thing to feel when his head was so full with all he had seen. He sank down, his belly touching the cold floor, and his front paws folded back on themselves. His eyes fell on the woodworm etchings that criss-crossed the floorboards in a frantic maze like the script of a long-forgotten language. Suddenly he realised the root of his loneliness: it wasn't just the loss of Eilidh, it was the suffocating burden of holding knowledge he could do nothing with. A beetle doesn't feel lonely under a rock because it cannot think. But Grimalkin could think and he could no more untether himself from his thoughts than a peacock could tear away the colour from its feathers. He was a light-house at sea with nothing but the frothing ocean. Realising this made him dizzy . . .

Who am I? he wondered, focusing on the clouds in the upper windowpane that had begun to race and twist.

He flinched. A pain had smarted along his back. Then an itch. He looked at his paw. To his astonishment, the little clutch of fleas which he had long suffered during the Victorian era had now returned and were happily nesting around a thinning patch of fur.

Is this it? Is this how it ends?

To his side, the couple snuggled on the sofa with the little cat snoozing between them. Now their bodies were beginning to blotch and stretch. Something was changing: the couple were moving gradually further and further away. Grimalkin felt hot and a little sick. But calm.

Slowly, one by one, his paws became limp, their talons gently unhooking from the pulp of the floorboards. His ginger flank and hooked tail melded that little bit closer with their smooth varnished form. The sounds around him seemed to stretch far off as if being heard along a great tunnel, and his purr, which usually reverberated throughout his whole body at times of rest like this, began to falter and drift to silence. *To sleep . . .* he thought. *My soul is tired. To sleep and not to dream any longer.*

And then two thoughts entered his head: one was of his mother; her eyes gummed together and her tortoiseshell stripes vibrant and gold as she licked him along his sticky fur as a newborn kitten. It was an image he had never had before during his whole life, but here it was now so clear and bright he could almost touch it. And then Eilidh . . . her smiling lips and rosy face looking down at him as he curled up near the fireside in 1902, tired and woozy.

Then at 8.07 on 8 September 2022, Grimalkin took his last breath. And all his thoughts and pains ceased and dissolved into air.

Grimalkin's Observations

Monarch: King Charles III.

Epilogue, December 2022

"SHALL WE TRY THE DUMMY?"

"Well, I think he's crying because he's hungry. Can you get the expressed milk?"

"Okay."

The Brass Man dropped his phone with a clatter and rose with a yawn. Over by the window, a mobile of lions and tigers swayed almost imperceptibly in the air current caused by his standing up. Beyond the window, a full moon cast a silvery ethereal light across the ancient sycamore tree, whose branches were dusted in a thin sheet of snow.

"But he was sick just now, wasn't he? Doesn't that mean he's full?"

"This is the hungry cry, though. I know the hungry cry."

"How do you know it's a hunger cry, he's only four days old?"

"Mother's instinct."

"Okay."

The Brass Man padded into the kitchen, his slippers speaking of his tiredness in their lazy *scuff-scuff-scuff* over the floor. The room was flooded with the colour and smells of Christmas; mince pies, cinnamon and sherry. Fairy lights looped around the shelves above the countertop accompanied by a clutch of *objets d'art* – a miniature Bovril tin, a model train and a series of cookery books arranged in order of colour. A bulbous turkey sat on the hob, covered with tinfoil. The Brass Man moved to the fridge and plucked out a bottle of milk. Had someone been present in the room at this point, they would have seen a gauntness to his face, the look of someone who has lost weight in a short amount of time, owing to a shock or dramatic change in circumstance.

"What time are they due, Otter?" he called through the flat.

"About eight, I think. Is the box room made up?" replied the girl.

"Yeah, it's ready."

The man left the kitchen clutching a bottle and met the girl emerging in the doorway to the back bedroom. Her cheeks were flushed red and her lips parted in a smile. "Can you take him while I do some pumping?" The man took the baby from her. "Oops, sorry, I forgot to say. I think he's just done a poo. I heard pipework."

The man laughed, looking down at the mewling little bundle in his arms, its body and limbs curled in on themselves like a tightly folded bud.

A tortoiseshell cat ran ahead of the three of them as they headed to the living room, past the stained-glass window over the front door, the stag looking drab and formless in the dark of the hallway.

"Tabby, you're behaving so strangely. Why are you always getting under our feet these days?"

They entered the living room. A little fire crackled in the grate comfortingly. All over the floor, baby paraphernalia lay strewn in semi-disorder: teddy bears, books, mobiles, nappies, rattles. Little did the family know of the history that had been snared within these four walls over the past 120 years: a history of people both great and ordinary, rich and poor, good and bad, despairing and triumphant.

"Oh, quick, quick, my boobs are leaking! Quick, Alex, pass him over!"

"Ah, right. God. Yes, okay. Here you go. I'll get the new nappies. They're in the back room in the hospital bag, yes?"

"Yes."

The Brass Man headed back down the hallway in big steps, the little cat darting ahead of him once again. In a flash, it disappeared into the gloom of the back bedroom. What the man didn't see (and would never know) was the strange way the moonlight caught the tabby cat's ginger flank in those few seconds before he himself arrived at the doorway. In those three lost seconds, he'd never know the strange commingling of supernatural forces that inhabited the little cat when its ginger flank met with the moon beam. But perhaps most remarkable of all, he would never spy the hulking form of a great cat perched on the roof of the opposite tenement, with the moon over its shoulder, a bead of white clearly visible on its chest despite the thick snow that began to fall all around.

"What on earth was that?!" cried the girl from the living room.

"It's Tabitha! It's mad ... She's just gone into the back bedroom and started yowling at the moonlight. Honestly, I'm starting to think this cat knows something we don't ..."

THE END

Acknowledgements

They say it takes a village to keep a writer sane while writing a book. It's true. From people in cafés, to extended family, to TikTok friends never met in person; I could thank so many. Without the following people, however, *The Ghost Cat* would probably never have happened ...

Firstly, the biggies: to my wife Ellie for her love, creative input and for enabling me to finish *The Ghost Cat* when Sasha was just weeks old. Not everyone would tolerate a fop bounding around polishing brass and scribbling notes with a baby in tow, but you did. You are hilarious, resilient and the finest mama to Sasha; I love you.

To my parents for always being there and giving me the kind of childhood where I could run amok with screwdrivers, dismantle mortice locks and hotwire the house's electricity to my attic den. Dad, you inspired my curiosity; Mum, you gave me my love of words and stories. You both gave me an obsession with period houses, a wholesome distrust of uPVC windows and a keen nose for paint-besmirched brassware. Thank you.

To the exemplary team at Black & White Publishing, particularly my editor Rachel Morrell for her warmth, creative input and reassuring WhatsApp messages at 8 p.m. Huge thanks as well to all my colleagues at Capital Theatres, Edinburgh for their enthusiasm for this project, particularly the wit and support of Richard Miller, Chris Townsend, Pab Roberts and all the Creative Engagement team.

To Lucy Ribchester for just about everything: telling me how to be a parent, making me howl, keeping me sane and fixing my plot conundrums. Enormous thanks to Janne Møller (my Danish guru), Cecilia Bennett and Emma Granberg for commenting on early drafts and ideas; you guys gave me the confidence to give this idea a go, and I'm hugely grateful.

To the TikTok community, for your love and devotion to the @housedoctoralex channel. To half-quote Sylvia Plath, you have split open my world like a ripe, juicy watermelon. I am a better person for your humour, knowledge and stories. Your presence in my life reminds me of the very best thing about being a writer: meeting cool new people.

For Sasha, for bounding into this world three weeks before the manuscript was due and thus obliterating any opportunity for procrastination. Your cheeks are softer than bao buns and make me smile every morning. Thank you for laughing at my impression of a drunk Count Dracula (and sleeping silently against my chest as I write this).

ACKNOWLEDGEMENTS

And to Tabitha, my "quality control", whose ginger flank inspired Grimalkin's own and who randomly hissed into the back bedroom one evening, thus giving me the idea for *The Ghost Cat.*

Alex Howard is an author, editor and theatre professional from Edinburgh. His TikTok page, @housedoctoralex, has nearly 300,000 followers and has been featured on television and in the national press.

A doctoral graduate of English literature, Alex wrote his first book *Library Cat* (Black & White Publishing) while completing his PhD. It won the People's Book Prize in 2017, and has been translated into French, Korean and Italian. He also writes poetry, which has appeared in *New Writing Scotland*, *Gutter* and *The London Magazine*, among others, while his academic book *Larkin's Travelling Spirit* (Palgrave Macmillan) was published in 2021.

Alex works at Capital Theatres as a Creative Engagement Coordinator and editor while renovating his Edinburgh tenement flat at weekends, with his cat Tabitha, son Sasha and wife Ellie.